SECRETS OF BEARHAVEN

BOOK ONE

SECRETS OF
BEARHAVEN

BOOK ONE

K. E. ROCHA

SCHOLASTIC PRESS / NEW YORK

Library of Congress Cataloging-in-Publication Data

Rocha, K. E., author.
  Secrets of Bearhaven / K.E. Rocha. — First edition.
      pages cm. — (Bearhaven)
  Summary: When Spencer Plain's uncle pulls him out of school, and they find themselves being chased by a strange car, Spencer does not know what is going on—but soon he is rescued from the woods by a bear, and taken to Bearhaven, a secret refuge his parents created, filled with bears who can talk, where, desperate to find his parents, he and a bear cub named Kate decide to take matters into their own hands.
  ISBN 978-0-545-81303-7 (hardcover) — ISBN 978-0-545-81313-6 (ebook) 1. Bears—Juvenile fiction. 2. Human-animal communication—Juvenile fiction. 3. Friendship—Juvenile fiction. 4. Rescues—Juvenile fiction. 5. Secrecy—Juvenile fiction. 6. Parent and child—Juvenile fiction. [1. Bears—Fiction. 2. Human-animal communication—Fiction. 3. Friendship—Fiction. 4. Rescues—Fiction 5. Secrets—Fiction. 6. Parent and child—Fiction.] I. Title.

PZ7.1.R637Se 2016
[Fic]—dc23   2015007040

10 9 8 7 6 5 4 3 2 1   16 17 18 19 20

Printed in the U.S.A.   23
First edition, January 2016

Book design by Nina Goffi

For Emma Dryden, Lorin Oberweger, and Elizabeth Grojean, for believing in wanmahai.

1

Roooaaaaaarrr!

Spencer Plain raced through the forest, his heart pounding. He dodged trees and skidded across patches of slick moss, trying desperately not to fall. Now was *not* the time to fall.

There was a bear behind him.

Spencer had taken one look at the bear, heard that ferocious roar, and set off running as fast as he could, but the huge animal was gaining on him. The ground was shaking and the thundering growls were getting closer.

With his eyes locked on an opening in the trees ahead, Spencer stumbled on a gnarled root and nearly lost his balance. *Keep running,* he told himself fiercely.

He had a feeling that if his uncle Mark were there, he'd be yelling at Spencer to *stop* running. But Uncle Mark couldn't tell Spencer to stop running, because Uncle Mark had left Spencer to the bears. Literally.

Crack!

A sharp sound echoed through the forest. A branch? A whole tree? He didn't dare look back to see what the beast had pulverized in its pursuit.

Spencer had never run so fast in his life, but he wasn't superhuman. He wasn't even fast enough to steal a base on his school's baseball team! His legs couldn't keep this up forever.

The path narrowed, and the opening in the trees that Spencer had been running toward was suddenly hidden behind more trees. Spencer started to panic.

Do bears eat humans? He searched his brain as he forced his body forward, his lungs burning. *Do bears eat humans?* Why couldn't he remember?

Spencer knew about bears. When he was little, his parents had told him ursine facts instead of bedtime stories, and sometimes he'd still recite those facts to himself when he couldn't fall asleep. He knew that black bears have forty-two teeth, that sun bears have the longest claws, and that brown bears can snatch jumping salmon right out of the air with their mouths. *But do bears . . . eat . . . humans . . . ?*

Spencer started to gasp for breath as he sensed the animal's massive body just behind him. And that's when he fell.

And kept falling.

He tumbled down a steep hill, kicking dirt up into his eyes and knocking against rocks and roots. He slid on his belly, awkwardly grasping for anything he might hold on to as he flew past, until finally the hill flattened and Spencer bumped to a stop.

He lay flat on his back, catching his breath and listening for signs of the bear. He didn't hear anything besides the sound of his own heavy breathing.

His whole body hurt. His parents had told him that if he ever took a bad fall, he should lie still and make sure nothing was broken. Now that he thought of it, wasn't that what you were supposed to do when you saw a bear in the wild—go totally still? He didn't think Mom and Dad had ever told him that, but then again he didn't think they'd ever told him to run for his life, either. "I should've just played dead," Spencer muttered as he assessed the pain in his body. "It would have been easier."

Spencer had gotten away. That's what mattered, he reminded himself. But just as he started to sit up, a huge black mass flew through the air and landed beside him with a ground-shaking crash.

The bear was back.

Snorting, it thrust its broad tan muzzle into Spencer's face. Terrified and frantic to get away, Spencer tried to get to his feet, but a massive paw landed heavily on his shoulder. He was trapped.

"Spencer Plain," the bear growled. "We have been expecting you."

2

Earlier that day . . .

Spencer was out of bed and dressed for school an hour before his alarm was set to go off. He was supposed to video chat with his parents over breakfast, and he had something important to talk to them about.

Too anxious to play video games or work on the computer that he'd taken apart and was supposed to rebuild from the pile of metallic rubble on his desk, Spencer picked up his laptop and went to the kitchen to find Evarita.

"Somebody's up early," Evarita said from behind a big mug of steaming tea as Spencer walked into the room. "Looking forward to seeing your parents?"

"Yup." Spencer set his computer down on the table. "I want to be ready when they call. Yesterday I only got to talk to them for a few minutes." He went to the fridge to pour himself a glass of milk. Evarita put down her mug and slid off the stool she'd been perched on. She opened and closed cabinets, pulling out bread and peanut butter for Spencer's breakfast.

Spencer liked Evarita. She was his parents' assistant, and she always stayed with Spencer when his parents traveled. He was too old for a nanny, but Evarita was more like family. She was funny and nice and was teaching Spencer to play the guitar while his parents were away, but he wished that she didn't have to take care of him so often. He wanted his mom to be the one making him peanut butter toast, and his dad to be sitting in the kitchen to greet him in the morning, not a million miles away in some hotel.

Spencer's parents had been gone for ten days already and hadn't told him when they'd be coming back. Usually they tried not to be away for more than a week at a time, but lately their trips had been getting longer. They were bear activists, which meant they knew everything about bears, but it also meant they had to travel around the world for their foundation, Paws for Peace, trying to make sure that no bears were being abused or mistreated.

Spencer knew that their work with bears was really important, and lots of kids at school thought his parents' jobs were cool, but sometimes Spencer wished that being an activist for bears meant that you just stayed home and wrote books about them.

Spencer was putting the milk back in the fridge when he heard the chirp of an incoming call from his laptop. He raced toward the table.

"Your parents can't wait to talk to you, either!" Evarita said, jumping back as Spencer barreled past her and into his seat. He clicked on the "accept call" button, and his parents' faces filled the screen.

"Hey there, early bird!" Spencer's dad said, smiling.

"Good morning, Spencer," his mom chimed in, leaning closer to the camera, a few strands of her sleek blond hair

5

falling out from behind the glasses she'd pushed to the top of her head.

"Hi!" Spencer answered happily. Out of the corner of his eye, he saw Evarita duck out of the kitchen, leaving him alone with his parents.

"Got your breakfast?" Dad asked. He looked tired, his face shadowed by stubble.

Spencer took a big bite of his toast. "Yup," he answered through a sticky mouthful. "Do you?"

Dad's arm reached out of the frame and then returned with a piece of peanut butter toast in hand. He answered with a big bite of his own.

"Cheers!" Mom tipped a glass of milk in Spencer's direction. As she lifted her glass to take a sip, a thin gold bracelet slipped down her wrist, and the familiar gold bear charm dangled into view. She'd worn that bracelet for as long as Spencer could remember, and while sometimes she stacked other bracelets around it, the one with the bear charm never left her wrist. He reached into the pocket of his cargo shorts and checked for his own lucky bear. He always carried it with him.

Spencer's bear wasn't gold like his mother's, and it wasn't a charm. It was a smooth, black jade figurine of a bear standing on its hind legs. His parents had given it to him three years ago on his eighth birthday, right before they'd started traveling so much. They'd explained that a bear on its hind legs was better equipped to be brave and strong because it could see, hear, and smell best that way.

Mom shuffled through a stack of papers with one hand and passed the glass of milk to Dad with the other. "What do you have going on today, Spencer?" she asked.

Spencer filled his mouth with toast, then gave a quiet, garbled answer. "I have to climb the rope in gym again."

His parents knew that he'd tried and failed, twice, to get to the top of the rope in gym class, but he didn't like to talk to them about his problem with heights. They wouldn't understand; his parents weren't afraid of anything.

"Well, third time's the charm, right, cub?" said Dad.

"I guess." Spencer shrugged and changed the subject. "I have to present my computer project on Monday. That's four days from now, and I'm not even close to done. I think I need you to help me, Dad."

"Four days, huh?" Dad leaned back in his chair and crossed his arms, the smile fading from his face. "You don't think you'll be able to get it into shape by then?"

"I don't know. It's really hard. I wrote everything down as I took the computer apart, and I drew diagrams, but I don't know . . ."

"Why don't you call Uncle Mark?" Mom asked, sliding her glasses back into place on the bridge of her nose and scanning one of the pages she'd been sorting.

Spencer didn't reply. If he asked, his uncle Mark would help him with anything. And his uncle *was* really good with gadgets and mechanical stuff, but that wasn't the point. He answered carefully, not wanting to sound like a baby. "I just want Dad to help me." He looked at his father. "I could do it better if you were here, Dad."

"I know, buddy, but we've got a few more days on assignment . . . It would be cutting it close—"

"You know we want to be there, honey," Mom cut in, "but the bears here—"

7

"Are more important," Spencer interrupted.

"Spencer! That's not at *all* what I was going to say!"

"It's not true, either." Dad leaned forward, putting his hands on either side of the laptop, as though by touching his computer he could touch Spencer.

"I have to leave for school," Spencer said abruptly, and disconnected the call. His laptop immediately began to chirp again, and for a moment Spencer hovered the cursor over his parents' incoming call. He'd be in trouble for hanging up on them, and he knew that he should apologize. Instead, he closed the screen.

Evarita poked her head into the kitchen. "Ready to go?"

"Almost." Spencer quickly reopened the laptop. A rotten feeling was already creeping into his stomach. He wanted to talk to his parents again, to apologize.

His laptop showed a missed call. He tried to reconnect, but his parents were already gone. He couldn't apologize even if he wanted to. Spencer slammed his laptop shut again. Maybe they didn't deserve an apology after all.

3

"Spencer!" Ramona practically shouted in Spencer's ear.

"What?" He turned his attention back to his two best friends, Cheng and Ramona, who were standing next to a row of lockers, both dressed in khaki-and-white school uniforms, staring at him. Was it that obvious he hadn't been listening?

"Are you nervous about rope climbing again?" Ramona sounded impatient. Spencer had known Ramona his whole life. She wanted him to get to the top of the rope as much as he did, even if it was just so they could all stop worrying that he would never pass sixth-grade gym class.

"I guess so." Spencer shrugged. He'd been dreading the climb since he'd gotten to school, and now that they were only minutes away from the start of gym class, his dread was getting way worse.

"Did you hear what I said?" Cheng asked. "About our game last night?"

Spencer hadn't heard, but he could guess what Cheng had said. His baseball-loving friend had already spent every free minute of the day rehashing each play of the Cougars' first game of the season.

"Look, it's your uncle!" Ramona exclaimed, starting to wave.

Uncle Mark? Spencer spun around. Sure enough, Uncle Mark was striding toward them. Mrs. Stewart, the school's secretary, charged along behind.

Spencer couldn't believe his luck. Was he going to get out of gym class? Maybe Mom and Dad felt as bad as he did about the way their call ended and had arranged for him to skip rope climbing!

"Spence!" Uncle Mark called. "Grab your stuff. We've gotta go. Now."

Out of the corner of his eye, Spencer saw Cheng and Ramona exchange a look. Was Uncle Mark just acting that serious so Mrs. Stewart would let Spencer out of school?

He gulped. He really hoped so.

Uncle Mark's red Porsche Cayman flew through the city streets, zipping between trucks and taxis at a speed that made Spencer check that his seat belt was fastened. He'd never seen his uncle drive so fast, and he wasn't enjoying it as much as he'd thought he would. The chance to miss school to race through the city should have been exciting, but right now his brain was too filled with questions for him to be having any fun. He'd been right that Uncle Mark's appearance just before gym class had something to do with his parents, but he'd been wrong about everything else.

"What's going on, Uncle Mark?" Spencer said, his voice coming out too high and a little shaky. "I talked to Mom and Dad this morning, and they were fine." It was one o'clock now. How could so much have changed in only seven hours?

"Same here," said Uncle Mark, slowing the car to idle at a red light. "But then I got a message from your mom around eleven, and I haven't been able to get in touch since."

"What *kind* of message?" Spencer asked. He looked out the window, trying to get his bearings, but they were stopped at an intersection in an unfamiliar neighborhood in the middle of a long stretch of brownstones. None of them offered any clues.

"Your parents made an important plan a long time ago, Spence. Your mom's message today was that I should put that plan in motion . . ." The light turned green and Uncle Mark shifted into gear, quickly pulling ahead of a garbage truck. "So here we are. In motion."

"What important plan?"

"I'm taking you to a safe place," Uncle Mark answered.

A safe place? None of this was making any sense, and the unrecognizable landscape whipping by them wasn't helping anything.

"Why wouldn't I be safe at school? Are Mom and Dad okay?" Spencer stared at his uncle, trying to gather more information from the expression on his face, but Uncle Mark just maneuvered the car around a slow minivan, looking as cool and collected as usual.

Uncle Mark took his hand off the gearshift and gave Spencer's shoulder a reassuring squeeze. "I'm sure they're fine, Spence."

Spencer didn't feel reassured.

"Then why—?"

"Spence, do you know what this is?" Uncle Mark interrupted, pointing toward the center console of the Porsche. Spencer looked over.

"The emergency brake?"

"Exactly. You know when to use it?"

That's easy, Spencer thought. "In an emergency."

"Yes and no. If the brakes fail, you'd use the emergency brake to stop the car. But ninety-nine percent of the time you use the emergency brake once you've already parked the car, to make sure that it doesn't roll away. How many cars have you seen just rolling around, crashing into things?"

"None." Spencer usually liked learning about cars, but right now he wished his uncle would just get to the point. "Uncle Mark, why do you have to take me to a safe place?"

"That's what I'm explaining, Spence. Ninety-nine percent of the time the emergency brake is just a precaution. This plan of your parents' is our emergency brake, and they asked me to pull it today. It doesn't mean anything bad has already happened, and it doesn't mean anything bad is *going* to happen, but we have to follow the plan, just in case."

Jostled by the speeding car, Spencer kept his eyes on the emergency brake, considering his uncle's words.

"Are Mom and Dad . . . *missing*?" He reached into his pocket and took hold of the jade bear, comforted by the familiar warmth of the smooth figurine.

"Not missing. *Out of communication* is a better way to put it," Uncle Mark said. "I'm taking you to a safe spot, and then I'm going to do what I can to get your parents home ASAP."

Spencer gripped the bear tighter and looked out the window. Gradually, the highway they were on shed lanes until it narrowed to just two, and then became a rough local road. It seemed like they'd been driving forever. How much farther could they be going?

"What are Mom and Dad afraid of?" Spencer finally asked, breaking the silence. That morning, Spencer hadn't thought that his parents could be afraid of anything, but now he felt like his world had turned upside down and anything was possible.

"Your parents are the bravest people I know, Spence. They're *not* afraid of anything, but they also know when to be cautious." Uncle Mark paused. "I don't have all the info right now, but what I *do* know is that your parents are really good at keeping bears safe, they're really good at keeping you safe, and they're really good at keeping each other safe. The best way we can help them get out of whatever trouble they might be in is by following the plan they made. We'll talk more when we get to—"

"To where?" Spencer asked.

"Hang on, Spence," Uncle Mark replied, his eyes on the rearview mirror. "There's a car behind us that I'd really like to lose. You buckled in?"

"Yeah." Spencer checked his seat belt for the millionth time. It wasn't until he felt the car accelerate to an even higher speed that he realized what Uncle Mark had just said.

"Wait, is someone *chasing* us?"

4

The old country road was rutted and bumpy, and even with Uncle Mark dodging the most treacherous potholes, Spencer's body jolted back and forth as they sped along. He kept his eyes glued to the side mirror. A black Corvette with no front license plate, the car behind them was pockmarked with dents and rust. Its windshield was tinted, and its muffler, by the sound of it, was completely gone. Spencer didn't like the looks of the Corvette, but he kept watching, and as it got closer, his heart started racing. Uncle Mark had turned on music, trying to cover the roar of the car behind them, but they weren't getting away.

The jade bear clutched in Spencer's sweaty palm was only barely keeping him from panicking.

"Change of plans, Spence," his uncle said calmly, watching the car behind them pick up speed. "I'd hoped to take you into safety myself, at least to make the introduction, but you're going to have to head into the forest without me so I can get this Corvette out of our hair."

"Introduction? To someone in the forest?" Spencer searched the wall of trees to their right. There was a field between the road and the forest, but the sun was setting, and it would be even darker once he got into the trees. Uncle Mark was just going to leave him here?

"When I find a place to stop the car, I want you to jump out."

"No!" Spencer shouted.

"It's okay. I know you're scared, but you have to trust me. This is all part of the plan. I promise." Uncle Mark grabbed Spencer's backpack from the backseat, pulled it forward, and dropped it into Spencer's lap. "Take your cell phone. I'll bring the rest of your stuff later, but you'll want to use your compass app once you get into the woods."

Spencer frantically dug through his backpack until he found his cell phone. "How will I know where to go?" He shoved the bag to the floor and the phone deep into his pocket with the jade bear.

Uncle Mark glanced into the rearview mirror. "There's someone waiting for you inside the woods. He's going to find you and take you the rest of the way. He's a good friend and he's going to take care of you. You can trust him just like you trust me, okay?"

The forest probably stretched for miles. Spencer imagined himself stumbling alone through the darkening woods, looking hopelessly for some stranger.

"Who *is* this guy? What if he doesn't find me? How will he know where I am?"

"He'll find you. He's got . . . heightened senses."

Spencer couldn't help but notice his uncle hesitate before going on. "And, Spence? This guy . . . he's . . . well, he's a bear."

"WHAT?" Spencer yelled so loudly that for a moment he didn't hear the un-muffled car behind them.

"Yes. He'll take better care of you than anyone else can right now." Uncle Mark scanned the forest. "He'll be north of here, so once you get into the woods, head north. He'll find you, I promise. You'll be fine."

His parents were nowhere to be found, he was about to be dumped on the side of the road in the middle of nowhere, and now his uncle had lost his mind.

"A *bear*?" Maybe he wasn't hearing things right. "Your *friend* who is supposed to keep me safe is a *bear*?"

"I know I probably sound crazy, but trust me. I'll meet up with you as soon as I can, and I'll explain everything." Uncle Mark caught Spencer's eye. He was serious.

"Listen to me. We're out of time. You just have to trust me." Uncle Mark's voice was unusually urgent. "I'm pulling over to the side of the road, and I want you to run as fast as you can into the woods. Do you understand?"

"No, I *don't* understand!" There was no way he was getting out of the car. There was no way he was going to let Uncle Mark leave him here. With a bear? No. Way.

"It's the emergency brake, Spence. Just stick to the plan. Trust your mom and dad." With that, the Porsche fishtailed to a stop, spraying gravel and kicking up a cloud of dust. Uncle Mark reached across Spencer to push open his door. "Run!"

The car behind them was getting louder. Uncle Mark wasn't giving him a choice, no matter how crazy this plan sounded.

Spencer leaped out and ran.

5

Wiry grass lashed Spencer's bare legs as he sprinted across the field toward the trees. Behind him, Uncle Mark revved the engine, and with another shower of gravel, the Porsche tore off down the road.

He was on his own.

He was halfway between the road and the trees, heading straight into a forest that housed at least one bear.

Bears didn't usually live in packs, but Spencer's parents had always told him that they were "social animals," just like kids at school: hanging out, doing things together during the day, but going home to different places, living separately. So that meant there was probably more than one bear in the forest ahead. He was just supposed to hope to find the friendly one first?

The roar of the Corvette reminded Spencer that no matter what he found in those woods, he needed to get into them, and fast. He glanced over his shoulder to see who he was running from, and the black car started to veer over to the side of the road.

Spencer dropped down onto his stomach. Whoever was in that car wasn't supposed to see him. He flattened himself against the cold ground, his shorts, shirt, and sneakers immediately soaking up the damp of the grass. Evarita wasn't going to be very happy when he got home. She hated laundry.

Of course, he had to get home for that to even matter.

With his face hovering inches from the ground and his nose filling with the thick smell of dirt and whatever was crawling around under him, Spencer willed the black car to keep going.

No such luck—there was a screeching of brakes, the sound of rubber on gravel, and the car ground to a stop.

Spencer lifted his head just enough to see a hulking man muscle himself out of the passenger-side door of the Corvette. Roughly the size and shape of a refrigerator, the man's huge body was enough to make Spencer's breath catch in his throat. A white football helmet gleamed on his head, hiding his face, and the man's huge hands were clenched in menacing fists. Spencer couldn't imagine why a man that big would need a football helmet anywhere but on a football field . . . unless he made a habit of smashing into things. Spencer didn't have to know who the man was, or what he wanted, to know that he was definitely creepy, and probably dangerous.

Spencer turned his attention back to the forest. Bear or no bear, he decided he would be safer in the woods, where he could duck behind something and hide, than in the middle of a field with a giant in a football helmet stomping around looking for him.

From where he lay on his belly, he didn't have far to go, but he couldn't risk jumping to his feet and running for it. Spencer pushed himself up to his hands and knees. Staying in the lowest crawl he could manage, he scrambled forward.

He expected to hear a shout, or powerful footsteps pounding behind him, but neither came. Instead, after a few moments, a car door slammed, the Corvette's engine gave a booming cough, and the car pulled away, crunching gravel as it accelerated. Spencer leaped up and dashed the remaining yards to the tree line. Hurtling between two enormous pines, he landed in the shadowed woods.

As soon as he was far enough into the forest that he couldn't see the road through the trees, Spencer leaned up against the thick trunk of an old oak. "Welcome to bear territory," he muttered, trying to catch his breath. This had to be better than the field with the football freak.

Spencer pulled out his cell phone. Great. No service. No chance of calling Uncle Mark or Evarita. He was really, really alone.

Spencer tapped the compass app and shoved his hand back into his pocket, grasping the jade bear. He needed all the help he could get. As he waited for the app to load, he listened to the sounds of the forest. Leaves rustled as a breeze blew through, chilling Spencer in his damp uniform. A bird dove down from a branch, and Spencer was so startled he almost dropped his phone, but the bird wasn't after him. Instead, it scooped a toad mid-ribbit from a root and carried it off. Spencer froze. *I am really in the woods,* he thought before shaking off the bird attack and refocusing on his phone. He knew that if the app didn't work without cell service he'd be in trouble, but he tried to push that thought out of his head. Without the compass he would never know which way north was . . .

Maybe he should have joined Boy Scouts with Cheng after all. Even Ramona would probably know something about navigating in a forest, with all the camping she and her family did during the summer. Cheng and Ramona were probably at home right now, doing homework or watching TV, something ordinary that didn't involve bears and being ditched in the woods. They'd never believe this . . .

The compass on Spencer's phone finally calibrated, and he pushed himself off the tree. He didn't like the sound of the rest of this "emergency brake" plan, but his only chance of finding the mysterious safe place was to go north, bear or no bear.

The compass read 272° west. Spencer turned to his right, eyes glued to the bright compass as the numbers ticked up and the marker moved along the circle's edge. When the compass registered 0° north, Spencer looked directly ahead of him. "Okay, let's get this over with," he muttered. Without looking back, he broke into a jog. He didn't want to still be in these woods when the sun went down . . . even if the only other option was meeting up with a bear.

6

Spencer wasn't sure how long he'd been running, but he'd referred to the compass over a dozen times. It said that he was still heading in the right direction, even though he didn't seem to be getting anywhere. The woods had gotten darker and more overgrown, but he hadn't seen any sign of the safe place Uncle Mark had talked about. No friendly bear had shown up to take him to safety, either, not that he minded waiting a little longer for *that* meeting.

The rotten feeling from that morning crept back into Spencer's stomach. He shouldn't have hung up on Mom and Dad, but he never thought anything would happen to them. They'd tried to call back! What if they'd wanted to tell him something important? What if he could have helped them get out of whatever trouble they were in now?

Spencer's thoughts were quickly brought back to the woods as he realized that he was running into a thickening fog. Wispy at first, it curled around Spencer in waves. There was something weird about this fog, though; it tingled a little, just like salt water did when it dried on his skin at the beach in the summer.

The fog hung so tightly around Spencer that he had to slow to a walk. He couldn't see the trees or even the ground anymore. He had to hold his phone close to his face to read the compass, its glow dulled by the murkiness around him.

Spencer's mouth filled with metallic mist. Coughing, he tasted the sharp tang of chemicals. Something was seriously wrong with this fog.

He pushed on, even though every step felt like walking through sticky mud, until his own voice surprised him. "I have to go home *right now.*"

No, that wasn't right . . . He *couldn't* go home. He had to go north—so why was he suddenly also sure that he needed to turn back? And why couldn't he make that thought go away?

Spencer tapped his flashlight app. The small beam of light popped on, but it only turned the fog into a wall of blinding white.

The fog again filled Spencer's mouth and lungs, making him double over in a fit of coughs. This time, though, Spencer realized that with his head bent toward the ground he could see better. The fog was thinner down there.

Crouching, he lifted his phone again, pointing the beam of light in front of him. The flashlight illuminated a clearing not far away with a tightly packed clump of trees beyond it. Would the bear be in there, waiting for him? Spencer wasn't sure it mattered anymore. At this point, whatever was in that clearing had to be better than the fog that was trying to suffocate him.

The fog prickled the back of his neck, but he stayed low and moved forward, keeping the flashlight trained on the path until he finally broke through the sheet of heavy gray mist.

At the edge of the clearing Spencer straightened. The nagging sense that he needed to go home was suddenly gone. He checked that his jade bear hadn't slipped out of his pocket, then looked at the compass. Dang! He was facing east now. The fog had him all turned around. Spencer turned to his left, his eyes locked on his phone screen.

After a few paces, the compass read 0° north. Ready to take off again, Spencer looked up. And there, across the clearing, looking him straight in the eye, was an enormous bear.

Roooaaaaarrr!

If that was the bear he was waiting for, there was no way he was going to stick around for an introduction. And if it wasn't—

Roooaaaaarrr!

And that's when Spencer turned and ran.

7

"Spencer Plain," the bear growled. "We have been expecting you."

Had he finally gone crazy, or had that bear just *said* something?

The dead weight of the bear's massive paw kept Spencer pinned in place as its snout prodded and sniffed at his arms and legs. Spencer wanted to close his eyes. He didn't want to see the bear's lethal-looking claws get even an inch closer, or its jaw open to reveal a mouthful of teeth, but he couldn't seem to look away. Fear kept his eyes open.

In the fur at the base of the bear's enormous neck rested a round device. Glowing green, the strange piece looked sort of like a speaker from the computer Spencer was supposed to repair by Monday.

The bear pulled back and looked Spencer over once more before removing its paw from Spencer's shoulder.

"Spencer Plain, are you injured?"

Now he was sure. That grave voice *had* come from the bear. No . . . the voice was coming from the machine at the bear's chest, and the words had followed a series of grunts, grumbles, and growls from the bear. It was some sort of technology—*some very cool technology,* Spencer found himself thinking—but he'd never heard of anything like it.

"Spencer Plain, have you injured your vocal cords?" The bear kept its eyes fixed on Spencer, and to Spencer's surprise, seemed to look impatient.

"How . . . how are you doing that?" he answered, and stared at the green light, waiting for it to reply.

The bear tapped his neck and growled.

The translation followed: "This is a BEAR-COM. Battery-Enabled Animal Reinterpreting and Communication device."

A bear language translator? No way! Did his parents know about this? Spencer wanted a closer look, but stopped himself from leaning toward it. It may be an awesome invention, but it was still attached to a bear. *A black bear*, Spencer thought.

A jagged furless patch ran the length of the animal's tan muzzle, and its nose, constantly sniffing, looked soft and leathery.

"If you aren't injured, then we had better be off." The bear stood on its hind legs and towered over Spencer.

"Wait—" Spencer protested, remembering the roar again. "If you're Uncle Mark's friend, then why did you—?"

"Apologies," the bear interrupted gruffly. "Our introduction did not go as planned. For security purposes, my BEAR-COM was off. I had intended to turn it on in time for our meeting, but it seems the fog was a problem for us both. I had *attempted* to say 'Don't run. I am here to take you to safety and am not interested in a chase at the moment,' but *clearly* it did not translate, so all you heard was my roar." With that, the bear bent down and began to open its mouth. The closer it got, the wider its jaws opened, until right above Spencer's head it revealed its forty-two gleaming teeth.

Spencer tried to scramble away, but before he could get his feet beneath him, the bear had clamped the back of his muddy shirt between its teeth and was lifting him off the ground.

8

Releasing Spencer's shirt from its mouth, the bear deposited him back on his feet.

"I assume you would prefer to walk," it said gruffly, and lumbered off before Spencer could reply. If the alternative was being carried by the scruff of the neck like a cub, Spencer agreed, he'd probably be better off walking. As long as he could keep up . . . The bear had already disappeared into the trees ahead, and Spencer had to break into a jog to catch up. Some guide this was. If he wasn't careful, he'd be left alone in the woods again.

Falling into place beside the bear, Spencer had to take three steps for every one of the enormous animal's.

"So," Spencer started awkwardly, a little winded but determined to hear more out of the BEAR-COM. "What's your name?" He stole a sideways glance at the green light of the device.

The bear suddenly stopped, staring straight ahead at what appeared to be an even denser wall of trees. Its nose twitched rapidly and it rose up on its hind legs, huffing and slowly turning its head from side to side.

Spencer had never seen trees growing so closely together. Their roots were fused, turning the ground into a treacherous knotty maze, and their trunks seemed to block every opening. How would they possibly get through? It would take forever! And Spencer was getting cold, his stomach starting to growl . . .

"I'm B.D." The bear interrupted Spencer's thoughts. "And now we're going up."

Spencer gulped. "Up?" He ran his eyes along the tall trunk of the tree in front of them.

"Yes," B.D. replied, and then dropped lightly to all fours and walked a few paces down the line of trees before singling one out and approaching it. "As in, up this tree."

The sight of B.D. scanning the dark canopy of branches and leaves far above made Spencer forget everything except the height of the tree and the hard rockiness of the ground.

"How far . . . *up?*" This was way worse than any rope-climbing class. At least in gym there were mats to soften the fall. "I don't think I can."

"Of course *you* can't," the bear huffed. "It's designed that way." B.D. lowered his body to the ground. "Climb on."

Spencer stared at the crouching bear. He couldn't decide which was worse, climbing the tree himself or holding on to a bear for dear life while the animal did the climbing.

"I am going to carry you up. Now, step on." B.D. extended one thick paw along his side.

Spencer shuddered. Uncle Mark hadn't mentioned anything about "up." Giving his jade bear one last squeeze, Spencer put both hands against B.D.'s massive flank. He stepped onto the thick black pad of the extended paw and, in one quick sweep, was hoisted up onto the bear's back.

For a moment, Spencer was able to imagine that he was little again, riding on the back of Ramona's Bernese mountain dog, Sheep. B.D.'s fur was just as soft as Spencer remembered Sheep's being, but those rides had been just for fun; this was very, very different.

"Grip my fur and hold on tight. You won't hurt me."

Clamping his legs against B.D.'s taut sides, Spencer grabbed fistfuls of the bear's fur, feeling the warmth of B.D.'s skin underneath. Then Spencer's body jolted forward as the bear launched himself at the tree.

9

Spencer squeezed his eyes shut and clutched the fur at the nape of B.D.'s neck. He didn't want to know how far below the ground really was. The thought of falling kept his whole body tensed in terror. He tried to take a deep breath, to make the fear go away, but his lungs were frozen and his mouth was filled with the bear's fur. Sputtering, he was about to ask B.D. how much farther when they lurched forward into what felt like a sudden burst of wind.

Opening his eyes, a scream immediately tore out of Spencer's mouth. The bear had leaped off the tree and into the open air!

Treetops spread in every direction, and a web of leaves and skinny branches obstructed his view. There was nothing for them to land on. Nothing to keep them from plummeting . . .

Thump.

They landed on something solid. Spencer gasped, his pulse thundering through his body. Peering over B.D.'s shoulder, he looked down. The bear's massive paws seemed to disappear beneath a layer of leaves, but through gaps in the leaves Spencer could see the ground far below. Which would mean they were standing on . . . thin air.

"What the . . . ?" Spencer started.

"All right. You can climb down now," B.D. said, crouching.

No way. Spencer was *not* about to find out if there was something real to stand on or not. "But there's nothing—"

"It's perfectly safe. Just slide off my back and stay close." B.D. shook his body, as though trying to shimmy Spencer down himself. Spencer clung to the bear's fur and swung around onto his stomach, slowly lowering himself toward . . . well, toward nothing. But then his sneakers touched a surface. He flattened his feet against it and looked down. "Whoa!" He couldn't see his feet anymore at all. They were covered by thick foliage, but he couldn't feel the leaves that surrounded his ankles. *What in the world?*

"We have to move quickly now," B.D. growled, and started forward. "It only covers the wooden bridge we're standing on."

"What does?" Spencer asked, and bent over to touch one of the leaves. It didn't feel like anything, like it wasn't even there, but Spencer's hand appeared distorted when he put it where the leaf seemed to be.

"The hologram. It's projected over the bridge to make it look like part of the canopy. This access point can't be located from above."

Of course! A hologram! Spencer had never seen one up close. He didn't know they could look so real. "And from below?"

"This bridge crosses the wall of the perimeter. As you saw, the trees that make the wall are tightly packed. If an intruder were to get through them, below where we are now, there are other lines of defense that would prevent them from looking up." B.D. lumbered forward, across what Spencer now knew was a hidden bridge. "Stay directly behind me," the bear went on, his impatience translating through the BEAR-COM. "We rarely use this entrance. Particularly with humans." B.D. increased his pace.

After a few more yards, B.D. stopped and rose onto his hind legs. He tugged aside an enormous tree limb to reveal a huge knothole. Getting a bit closer, Spencer saw that the knothole was actually an entrance, and apparently one that B.D., nudging Spencer forward, wanted him to go through.

"What's next?" Spencer muttered, stepping through the knothole and onto a grated metal floor. "A tree-shaped rocket ship?" The tree trunk had been totally hollowed out, its walls smooth, and there was plenty of space for him and B.D. inside. He looked back through the knothole, expecting the bear to follow. Instead, the bear touched a claw to a yellow button atop his BEAR-COM and began to grumble. "Professor Weaver, we're all set. I'll stand guard."

The floor beneath Spencer began to vibrate. "Wait!" he yelled, and tried to scramble back out of the knothole. B.D. was supposed to keep him safe! He couldn't just leave him now!

But it was too late. The platform was dropping down into the depths of the tree, taking Spencer with it into darkness.

10

The platform shuddered to a halt, throwing Spencer off balance. Putting an arm out to catch himself, he misjudged in the dark how far he was from the wall and toppled over onto the metal floor. Just then, a door slid open behind him, and the hollow tree was filled with a golden light.

"He's here!"

"Yes, but let's give him a moment. Looks like he's taken a spill."

Spencer didn't move. He recognized the slight electronic twang in the voices behind him. More BEAR-COMs. Which meant . . . more bears.

"I'm going to see—"

"Kate Dora Weaver, you get back here!" Spencer heard a scuffle, and then the approaching *thump-thump, thump-thump* of footsteps. The light from the doorway was blotted out as the growing shadow of a bear rose up onto its haunches, blocking his only exit.

After everything he'd been through, Spencer wasn't about to be delivered like a fish fillet to a sleuth of bears. Leaping to his feet, he spun around to face the looming beast and raised his arms to defend himself.

To his surprise, it wasn't an enormous bear that stood at the tree's entrance at all, but a chestnut-colored cub. Dropping down to all fours and shuffling back a few paces, the cub seemed just as startled by Spencer's sudden movement as he was by its unexpectedly small size.

"Give him some space, Kate, dear," a voice called. Spencer looked past the cub to a clearing lit by lanterns that reminded him of street lamps, and five bears staring back at him.

"I'm just *looking*," the cub said over her shoulder. She loped back and forth in front of Spencer, then sat back on her hind legs and peered at him expectantly. Her BEAR-COM glowed green, and seemed to be sparkling. Spencer saw it was dotted with pink heart-shaped crystals. "I'm Kate and I smelled you an hour ago!" she exclaimed.

An hour ago? If her sense of smell was that good, maybe she could help find his parents! Maybe if she could sniff them out . . . Dropping his arms, Spencer relaxed out of his defensive pose and stepped into the clearing, not taking his eyes off the boisterous cub. For the first time since leaving school that afternoon, he didn't feel afraid. Spencer could barely smell Kate's earthy animal odor now, and they were only a few feet apart.

A much larger black bear with tan jowls started toward Spencer. "Wait with your brothers now," it murmured, passing Kate.

"But, Dad—"

"Now," the bear replied firmly.

Kate dropped to all fours. "I just wanted to say hi." She pouted and retreated to join the others, dragging her paws dramatically with every step.

The large bear turned to Spencer. "Spencer Plain, we're happy to see you've arrived safely. Welcome. I'm Professor Weaver."

On Professor Weaver's chest, right below his BEAR-COM, was a white patch of fur in the shape of a triangle. *A blaze mark,* Spencer thought, comforted by the familiar bear fact. Mom called these marks distinguished, and Dad called them bear tattoos, but either way, Spencer had always loved bears with blaze marks, knowing that they were rare. He looked hopefully back at Professor Weaver; maybe these bears really *could* help him.

"Hi," he said tentatively. As soon as he'd spoken, another bear rushed forward as though drawn to the sound of his voice. Slightly smaller than Professor Weaver, this bear's fur shone silvery blue in the lantern light.

"Oh, Spencer," the bear gushed through the BEAR-COM in a voice Spencer thought sounded female. "You're all grown up!" She tucked her head right beside Spencer's, lightly resting what would fit of her copper-colored muzzle on his shoulder for a brief moment. He couldn't help but think that people had it all wrong—*this* was a bear hug. "We haven't seen you in so long, dear." She pulled back and looked him over.

"*Seen* me?" For the millionth time that day, Spencer got the feeling that everyone knew a whole lot more about his life than he did, and he didn't like it one bit. How could these bears know him?

"Of course, you wouldn't remember. You were so very, very young then," the female bear rushed on. "I'm Bunny Weaver. You've met our youngest, Kate, and that's Winston and that's Jo-Jo, two of our boys." When their mother said their names, the two bears bobbed their heads in greeting. Kate had bounded forward at the sound of hers.

"Can we take him home now? Can we? Please?"

Home? Was the safe place Uncle Mark had promised Spencer a cave full of bears?

"Yes, Kate," Professor Weaver answered. "I think it's about time we did. You've had a long day, haven't you, son?"

Spencer nodded. He was exhausted and getting colder. At this point, a pile of leaves in a warm, dry bear cave didn't sound so bad. "Will Uncle Mark be there?"

"He'll be here soon, dear," said Bunny as the bears turned to leave the clearing.

Without hiding his disappointment, Spencer looked to Professor Weaver, hoping for more information. The large black bear nodded and lifted up onto his haunches, his snout rapid-fire sniffing. He turned his head from side to side and then lifted a claw to the yellow button atop his BEAR-COM. "B.D., an update on Mark's location, please."

Spencer held his breath, afraid of what he might hear next. What if Uncle Mark hadn't been able to get away from the giant in the Corvette?

Just then a gravelly voice transmitted through the BEAR-COM. "Smelled him at the northern port about an hour ago, Professor." It was B.D. "Nothing since." *Nothing since?*

Professor Weaver didn't look concerned. "Thank you, B.D. I gathered the same. He's boarded the TUBE, then."

"I can confirm," came B.D.'s reply.

"Only if there's a problem. We're taking Spencer home now." Professor Weaver dropped back to all fours.

"Your uncle's coming," he said to Spencer. "Not far behind—"

"Come *on*!" Kate shouted, dashing out ahead to lead them down a path through the trees. The rest of the Weavers fell into step behind her, and wearily, Spencer followed.

The path, dotted with golden lamps every few yards, wound to the base of a steep hill. Up ahead, Kate let out a set of untranslated growls that reminded Spencer of the way Evarita would hum to herself. He'd never heard of bears humming, but after the day he'd had, Kate could pull out a ukulele and begin to play and it wouldn't surprise Spencer. The cub circled back to pad beside him. "Almost there!" she encouraged, nudging him forward with her muzzle.

In the darkening evening, the grass was slick with dew, making the hill nearly impossible for Spencer to climb, but he had made it almost to the top when he lost his footing and began to slide. Exhausted, he expected to slip all the way back down the incline, but with a sudden jerk, he felt himself reverse directions. Spencer was being dragged up, his shirt clamped roughly between Kate's teeth.

"Oh, honey, no," cried Bunny Weaver when she turned to see Kate clumsily deposit Spencer on top of the hill. "You need to be gentle, remember?"

Kate looked from Spencer to her mother. "He was falling and I was helping," she mumbled in protest, hanging her head.

Shaky and definitely bruised, Spencer got to his feet. "Don't worry, I'm fine." Just then, Jo-Jo lightly headbutted Spencer's shoulder, directing him toward a space in the trees.

"Check it out," Jo-Jo said, before lumbering through the space, Winston close behind. After an encouraging nod from Bunny, Spencer followed, but stopped short on the other side of the trees. A valley lit by moonlight stretched out before him, and in the valley, an entire town.

11

Moss-covered homes spread out in widening crescent-shaped rows, their curved roofs transforming the valley below into a sea of green waves. Lantern-lit brick pathways spiraled throughout, dividing the town into sections, like a great, glowing honeycomb. A broad river snaked through the valley, as dark and gleaming in the moonlight as the black jade in Spencer's pocket, and a path running from a dock at its edge encircled the perimeter of the town before cutting directly to its center. A round clearing stood in the very middle of the illuminated network below, bordered by a string of stone buildings, and at its center, atop a long metal pole, flew two flags. Spencer could just make them out, drifting back and forth in the darkness.

Professor Weaver emerged through the break in the trees and stood beside Spencer. "Welcome to Bearhaven," he said, throwing a heavy paw around Spencer's shoulders. Bunny and Kate filed in around them, but Spencer didn't take his eyes off the scene below.

In the combined light of the moon and hundreds of lanterns were bears. Lots and lots of bears.

"What *is* this place?" Spencer whispered.

"This is our home," answered Bunny warmly. "And yours, for the time being."

"Home, home, home," sang Kate as she started down the hill toward Bearhaven, her brothers already far ahead and disappearing along one of the town's arching paths. Spencer hesitated. *His* home?

"Are . . ." he began awkwardly, not wanting to be rude. The Weavers were wonderful and all, but . . . "Are all of the bears down there—"

"Like us?" Professor Weaver offered.

"Yeah, or . . . safe?"

"Of course they are, Spencer! You're safe here with us," Bunny quickly replied, but Spencer saw her cast a sideways glance at her husband before adding, "With *all* of us."

As the Weavers started down the hill, Spencer reached into his pocket to grip his jade bear. If his parents and uncle knew about this place, why had they never mentioned it? Just once he wished someone would tell him the whole story.

Spencer saw Kate turn back, and in the hopes of avoiding another meeting with her teeth, he jogged down and joined the Weavers. Together, they entered the streets of Bearhaven.

The homes were set into the earth and looked like rounded caves, varying in height and shape as the land they were built into rose and fell. Spencer noticed that each one had a wide wooden door etched with claw marks and a circular window cut roughly into its upper half. Chimneys poked out of the rooftops, many of them puffing smoke, and lanterns hung beside the doorways, casting light over the stone benches or collections of plants and rocks that the bears had arranged in front of their homes.

As they drew closer to the center of Bearhaven they began to pass more and more bears. All of the bears wore BEAR-COMs, and many nodded to Spencer and the Weavers, murmured greetings, or stopped to watch, their expressions stoic and mysterious.

"There will be plenty of time for tours and introductions, Spencer," Bunny explained, shuffling him steadily forward. "For now it's time we got you home."

Turning onto one of the paths that bordered Bearhaven's center, Spencer noticed shops, a meetinghouse, and a restaurant called Raymond's Café.

Outside of Raymond's, a couple of bears sat on stone benches around a wooden table. The bears were so deep in conversation that when Spencer passed, flanked by the Weavers, they didn't seem to notice, but continued to grumble to one another. To Spencer's surprise, he couldn't understand anything they were saying. Their BEAR-COMs were dark. No translations came through at all.

Spencer turned to ask Professor Weaver about the silent BEAR-COMs, but the older bear was already a few paces ahead, greeting a scrawny bear in a hooded green cloak.

"Evening, Yude," Professor Weaver said to the approaching bear.

"*Nagauio,*" the bear answered, before meeting Spencer's gaze with a cold stare.

Uneasy, Spencer stepped closer to Kate, giving the bear called Yude extra room to pass. He'd seen dozens of bears since entering Bearhaven, but none of them had looked at him like that.

"Wait till you see where we live, Spencer!" Kate didn't seem to notice Yude as he continued down the path, but Spencer felt a lasting chill from the cloaked bear's gaze. It was clear that Yude didn't want anything to do with him, but why? Spencer knew that bears could be unpredictable and dangerous, especially when provoked, but he hadn't done anything to provoke this bear.

"Doe Ray MEEE!" Spencer's thoughts were interrupted by the sound of Kate's voice booming beside him. When she finished her off-pitch trill, she said, "And *that's* why they call us the Weaver Family Singers." She looked very pleased with herself.

"Uh . . . what?" Spencer gaped at her.

"The Weaver Family Singers. We're like a *band*!" Kate made a series of small sniffs and huffs. Nothing came out of the BEAR-COM, but looking at the wide smile on the cub's face, and her bouncing gait, Spencer realized that Kate was giggling. He'd have to ask her what the Weaver Family Singers was later.

Up ahead, Professor Weaver was pushing open the door of one of the domed dwellings. Spencer squinted at the wooden door, examining the claw marks that seemed to slash threateningly across its surface. *It's a design!* he realized. The claw marks weren't accidental or scary, as he'd first thought when he noticed that they marked every door in Bearhaven. Instead, they seemed to be a carefully carved design.

"Come on, you two!" Bunny called. She stepped into Spencer's view of the door and turned to usher him and Kate into the Weavers' home.

12

"We're here!" Kate sang as she burst into the house. "Aldo! Lisle! I brought Spencer Plain!"

Stepping through the doorway, Spencer braced himself to meet more bears. Instead, he was relieved to find Bunny quieting Kate. "Aldo and Lisle aren't here. We didn't want to overwhelm Spencer tonight." Turning to Spencer, she added, "You'll meet the rest of the family tomorrow."

The rest of the family? *How many more Weavers could they fit in this place?* Spencer thought, then realized his mistake.

He was standing in the entryway of an enormous amber-colored room. Professor Weaver was stoking a pile of glowing embers in a fireplace so big that Uncle Mark could park his Porsche in it. A fluffy moss-colored carpet spread across the floor, and four oversized couches were positioned to face the hearth. Spencer briefly wondered what a bear looked like sitting on a couch, but waved the thought away, guessing it wouldn't take long for him to find out.

Along one side of the room stretched a kitchen. Stone counters varied in height and depth, as though they'd been carved from a boulder that was there long before the house, maybe even before Bearhaven. Shelves climbed the walls, piled high with wooden platters, jars of thick-looking liquids, and bowls full of nuts and berries. Spencer couldn't tell if any of the shiny devices throughout the kitchen were actually used for cooking, but decided that with the BEAR-COMs, state-of-the-art culinary equipment would fit right in here.

Through a curved doorway on the far side of the room, Spencer could just make out a set of broad steps leading down, deeper into the ground.

Of course! The bears' home was built *down,* not up. The rows of rounded roofs that had looked so small from above were just the beginning. He'd only seen the very surface of Bearhaven.

Professor Weaver stepped back from the blazing fire. "Why don't you come sit down, son," he said. "I'm sure that Bunny wants to get you straight to bed, but something tells me you're not going anywhere until your uncle arrives."

Spencer nodded, glad that he wouldn't have to wait in some guest room alone, and went to settle himself on a couch patterned with overlapping leaves. Kate followed and flopped down onto the carpet in front of the fireplace, stretching out on her back.

"You must be starving, Spencer," Bunny said, but before Spencer could answer her, a sharp knock rattled the door. Spencer jumped, his bare arms and legs suddenly covered in goose bumps as the memory of Yude's cold stare raced into his head. Professor Weaver rose on his hind legs, his head only a few inches from the ceiling when he stood at his full height, and Bunny bustled to the door.

Spencer reached for his jade bear, pushing Yude's image out of his mind. There was nothing to be afraid of. He was safe here, he told himself, with a stone bear in his hand and a real one standing between him and whoever was out there.

"Spence!"

Uncle Mark stood in the threshold, a duffel bag in one hand and Spencer's backpack in the other. He winked at Spencer. "I see you found the place." He dropped the bags, crossed the room, and pulled Spencer up from the couch into a hug.

Stepping back, Uncle Mark looked him over. "I'm glad to see you're still in one piece. I know I've got some explaining to do." *Some* explaining to do? That was an understatement.

"How are Mom and Dad?" Spencer blurted out.

"Why don't we all sit down," Uncle Mark said, dropping onto the leafy couch. "Professor, Bunny, you'll need to hear this, too."

Spencer sank back down onto the couch next to Uncle Mark, Professor Weaver reclined on a couch facing them, but Bunny, crossing the room, suddenly cried, "Kate! That's not yours!"

Everyone turned to see Kate pull her head out from the depths of Spencer's backpack, a brown paper bag hanging from her mouth. Ignoring her mother's glare, Kate trotted over to Spencer. She dropped the bag in Spencer's lap.

"I smelled it!" she told him cheerfully.

Surprising himself, Spencer laughed. "My lunch!"

He was exhausted and anxious to hear news about his parents, but he was also starving. He'd forgotten all about the extra peanut butter sandwich that Evarita had tossed into his backpack that morning. "Fuel for the rope," she'd called it.

"Thanks, Kate," he said.

"You *said* he was hungry!" Kate bounded out of the room before Bunny could reply.

Unwrapping his crushed, soggy sandwich, Spencer saw Bunny shoot Professor Weaver a look as she sat down beside him. The professor stifled a chuckle, then turned his attention to Uncle Mark, an expression of total seriousness on his face.

"What can you tell us, Mark? How are Jane and Shane?"

"Where are they?" Spencer asked through a mouthful of sandwich. Uncle Mark ran a hand through his hair and turned to face Spencer. And at that moment, Spencer knew. They hadn't pulled the emergency brake as a precaution. Something was really, really wrong.

"Spencer, your dad's been captured."

13

"Spencer, dear, are you all right?" Bunny exclaimed.

Spencer was coughing, choking on bread and peanut butter. Gulping for air, he finally managed to swallow. "Maybe it's too much," Bunny said protectively.

"No!" he gasped. "I'm okay." But he was definitely *not* okay. Dad was . . . captured?

"Do you want me to go on, Spence?" Uncle Mark asked gently. Spencer nodded, setting the sandwich, half-eaten, in his lap.

"He was taken from the mission site around ten o'clock this morning. Your mom wasn't with him at the time, but she's gone undercover so that she can stay close by."

"Where are they?" Spencer asked again.

"We don't know." Uncle Mark ran a hand through his blond hair once more. That was the only way Spencer had ever been able to tell that his uncle was upset. Catching his eye, Uncle Mark dropped his hand, quickly regaining the air of total coolness that Spencer was so used to.

"The rescue mission seemed to have been going fine. Then things went haywire. There's no way of knowing when Jane will be able to send further communication. Obviously, the security surrounding whoever's behind all of this is higher than any of us had expected."

"Behind all of what?" Spencer broke in, getting the feeling that they were talking about more than just his missing parents. Uncle Mark hesitated, and then seemed to decide against telling Spencer that he'd explain later.

"For the past several years while your parents have been on rescue missions, they've also been working to uncover who's behind a large network of bear abuse." *Years?* All of this had been going on for *years?*

"We think they've gotten much closer, as of late," Professor Weaver added, rising off the couch and starting to pace behind it. "We're well equipped, Spencer. We're going to bring your parents home safely."

"Of course we are!" Bunny assured him, as though any alternative wasn't worth considering. But it was all of those alternatives that kept popping into Spencer's head, bringing him closer and closer to really freaking out.

"Spencer, you look absolutely exhausted," Bunny said with concern. She stood and dropped to all fours. "It's time we got you out of those filthy, wet clothes and into bed."

"But—" Spencer tried to protest. Uncle Mark had promised to tell him everything! Before he could say so, Bunny was beside him, using her strong muzzle to gently push him off the couch and onto his feet.

"No buts, dear. I promised your parents that I'd look after you, and that's exactly what I intend to do. Off we go." Spencer felt himself being carefully navigated toward the stairs, but he wasn't ready to leave Uncle Mark yet. He would never be able to sleep, not with so many questions unanswered. He tried again to make Bunny wait.

"Bunny's in charge, Spence," Uncle Mark chimed in. "But we can talk before you go to bed. I'll meet you in your room."

Before Spencer could say anything else, Bunny had him descending the stairs, which were almost more than his exhausted body could handle.

Bear-sized, each step demanded four strides for Spencer to cross, and the drop from one to the next took him as far as three steps at home would. Patiently, Bunny followed along behind.

When Spencer dropped down off the last step, he found himself in a long hallway. Beehive-shaped lights lined the walls, illuminating the cavernous space, and doors stood open along both sides. As he followed Bunny down the hall, she pointed out various things about each room they passed.

Spencer kept hold of his jade bear and swiveled his head back and forth, trying to be polite. He could tell that Bunny wanted to make him feel at home or take his mind off his parents, or both, but Spencer didn't need to feel at home here. He *had* a home, and nothing could distract him from the fact that he didn't know when he'd see his parents again.

Voices spilled out into the hallway from the family room as they passed. "It'll take more than that to be the Salmon King!" someone taunted. Spencer was surprised to recognize the sounds of a video game being played. Interested despite his determination not to be, he stopped to look in.

Winston and Jo-Jo were tussling in the middle of the large room. Surrounded by slouchy chairs and oversized toys, both wore sleek silver helmets and gloves that looked like oven mitts. On a gargantuan screen in front of them, two animated 3-D bears fought to catch salmon as they leaped from a raging waterfall.

"I am the Salmon *King*!" Winston howled, ramming his shoulder into Jo-Jo's.

"You'd be lucky to catch your *reflection*," Jo-Jo answered, darting away.

On the screen, the bears fought over the leaping fish. Each time a virtual bear hugged a salmon to its belly, the fish glowed silver, then transformed into a skeleton before evaporating into a sparkling mist.

"Ten more minutes, boys," Bunny called over Spencer's shoulder as she passed.

"Winston's going to bed hungry!" Jo-Jo replied without taking his eyes off the game. His on-screen bear snatched another salmon.

As Spencer turned to leave, Winston called out, "Come play, Spencer!"

"Tomorrow," Bunny said from the hall.

"Thanks," Spencer added. "I'll definitely play tomorrow."

Bunny was standing beside a closed door, waiting for him. "And this is your room," she said as he approached. "It's been your mom's project for some time now."

His mom? What could Mom have to do with a guest room in the Weavers' house? Bunny opened the door to reveal Spencer's room.

Spencer gasped.

"She wants you to feel like you're home."

14

Spencer stepped into a room that was *identical* to his bedroom at home. The same blue-and-silver comforters were on the bunk bed, and a Cougars baseball pennant hung above the top bunk, just like his had for years. The pictures of race cars that Spencer had taped to his wall at home were arranged in the very same order on the wall above the same white desk, and his favorite books and games filled the bookshelves.

Mom had done all of this for him. He imagined her taping up the pictures herself, adding books to the bookshelf here whenever he got new books at home. He examined the short length of rope that was looped around one post of the bunk bed. It looked identical to the one at home, but Spencer could tell it wasn't the one Dad had used to teach him knot tying. He'd practiced on that rope until it was soft and frayed. Still, it seemed like Mom had tried to break in this length of rope herself, matching it as well as she could to the one that Spencer knotted and untied whenever he couldn't fall asleep. He should never have said that Mom cared more about bears than about him. Even when she was here, surrounded by bears, she'd been thinking about him.

He went to the window, where the same blue curtains hung, the shade drawn behind them. *Aren't we underground?* he thought as he pushed one of the curtains aside and peeked behind the shade. *Yup. Belowground.* Behind the curtain there was a solid white wall, but it didn't matter. With the curtains closed, the room looked exactly like home.

"There are clothes in the dresser for you," Bunny said after giving Spencer a moment. He walked over to the familiar white dresser and opened the top drawer. On top of the stack of clothes sat a letter. "Is there anything else you need, dear?"

"No," he answered quickly. "Thank you," he added, turning back to Bunny.

"All right, then," Bunny said, and dropped her head to Spencer's shoulder for just a moment, her soft fur grazing his neck. "Sweet dreams." Her voice was melodic, like she was singing a lullaby. "Sweet dreams."

After Bunny left and shut the large door behind her, Spencer picked the letter out of the drawer. He opened the envelope and unfolded the single sheet of paper, realizing at once that he'd seen it before. It was an exact copy of the letter Mom had given him on his eighth birthday, explaining why she and Dad were giving him the black jade bear. He put the letter back in its envelope before crossing the room and stuffing it under the pillow on the top bunk. He would read it later, before he fell asleep. Uncle Mark would be coming in any minute, and he needed to change into clothes that didn't look and feel like they'd been chewed up and spit out by a . . . well, by a bear.

Spencer pulled on a pair of gray sweatpants and a *Car and Driver* T-shirt just like the one he had at home. As soon as he'd transferred his jade bear from the dirty heap of his school uniform and into the pocket of his sweatpants, there was a knock on the door, and Uncle Mark poked his head in.

"Not too shabby, huh?" he said as he pushed open the door and came in. "Your mom did a great job. You like it?"

"Yeah, it's cool," Spencer said.

Putting Spencer's backpack down beside the desk, Uncle Mark tossed his own duffel bag onto the bottom bunk. "How are you holding up, Spence?" he asked, shrugging out of his leather jacket.

"Uncle Mark!" Spencer exclaimed. *Holding up? Is Uncle Mark serious?*

"Right." Uncle Mark hung his jacket on the back of Spencer's desk chair, and then pulled it out to sit. "Might as well get comfortable." He nodded to the bunk bed. Spencer pushed the duffel bag aside and sat down. As soon as he had, the questions started tumbling out.

"How'd you get away from that car? Do you think Dad's okay? Wherever they're keeping him . . . He'll be all right, right? Until—"

"One thing at a time, Spence. I managed to outpace the Corvette long enough to make it into a hidden railway tunnel. It's another entry point for Bearhaven, and it's big enough to pull the Porsche into, but I had to lose the Corvette first. As for your dad, he'll be all right until we can get him out of there. Your mom is going to do everything she can to make sure of that." Uncle Mark sat back in his chair, looking at Spencer solemnly. "Why don't I start at the beginning."

"Okay," Spencer answered, not sure he even knew what the beginning was.

"Honestly, Spence. I never agreed with your mom's decision to keep Bearhaven from you," he started. Sometimes Uncle Mark and Mom didn't agree on things, but Spencer figured that was just typical brother/sister stuff. He didn't know it had anything to do with him. "She kept it secret for so long in order to protect you and to give you a normal life. But Bearhaven is in your blood. It was just a matter of time before—"

"But what *is* Bearhaven?" Spencer cut in. "And how did these bears become—"

"These bears? It's a long story."

15

"Back when your mom, dad, and I were in college together, Gutler University kept three bears on campus as mascots," Uncle Mark began. "They were treated badly, and that didn't sit well with us. Your dad and I were in the science department. We'd gotten close to one professor, a brilliant bear biologist and a really wonderful guy named Weaver. Aside from his work at the university, the professor had been working on his own secret project, and when we went to him with our concerns about the bears, he finally revealed the details of his work to us."

Uncle Mark leaned forward in his chair, resting his forearms on his thighs. There was excitement in his tired eyes.

"With the help of a bear that he'd found as a cub and raised in his home, Weaver had developed the very first prototype of the BEAR-COM. When we went to see the technology, and when we met his bear, we all realized that there was no going back. Weaver and this bear were able to communicate!"

"Weaver?" Spencer broke in, the name finally clicking into place. "*Professor* Weaver?"

"Right. Our professor at Gutler passed his name on to his cub and secretly designed the BEAR-COM with the bear's help. That bear is the Professor Weaver you met tonight."

"No way!" Spencer exclaimed. "And the mascots?"

"We were able to spring two of the mascot bears from Gutler, and with the help of the Professors Weaver and their BEAR-COM, we set up Bearhaven."

"So you and Mom and Dad and a bear *made* this place?"

Uncle Mark nodded. "For the bears from Gutler, but also as a haven for other bears that have been rescued from dangerous situations. Over the years, hundreds of abused bears have been brought to Bearhaven to recover. If the bears want to be restored to their natural habitat, to live like other bears in the wild, they can get treated here first, then they move on. Some, like the Weavers, choose to stay in the hidden safety of Bearhaven and help other bears in trouble."

Spencer couldn't believe it. Why wouldn't Mom and Dad want him to know that they were doing something so awesome to help bears? He tried to imagine his parents at Gutler, making their very first rescue—

"Wait, what happened to the third bear at the university?"

"There were two brothers and a sister. We got the two males out, but . . ." Uncle Mark paused. "We couldn't get the female out quickly enough. The Gutler bear handler recaptured her. It was awful. We heard the bear eventually escaped, but we don't know if that's true. She certainly never made it to Bearhaven, and we never saw her again."

Uncle Mark stood up and started to pace around the room.

"Since then, our work has been rescuing bears and guiding them here. Unfortunately, there are a lot of bears out there that need rescuing, and a lot of bad people who don't want someone just swooping in and taking their bears. These bears can bring in a lot of money, Spence, and oftentimes the people making that money don't consider the animals . . . Well, you understand."

"Yeah, I understand," Spencer said. He'd been hearing about animal rights his entire life. He knew how badly some zoos and circuses treated their bears—and all their other animals, too. He could see why Bearhaven needed to be so well hidden.

"So Mom and Dad have . . . enemies?"

"You could put it that way," Uncle Mark answered carefully.

The giant in the football helmet suddenly popped into Spencer's head. If his parents had enemies, did that mean *he* had enemies? "Like the people in the Corvette?" he asked, afraid to hear the answer.

"Yes. That was Margo Lalicki behind the wheel, and her brother, Ivan. Margo was the bear handler at Gutler. She's a cold, uncaring woman without a good bone in her body. When we rescued the bear mascots, the abuse they'd suffered made the news. Margo was fired from Gutler because of it. She's never forgiven us."

"So Ivan's the guy in the football helmet?"

"You saw him?"

"Just for a minute," Spencer admitted.

"He's all brawn and very few brains, if you know what I mean." Uncle Mark shook his head. "Don't worry about the Lalickis. We can handle them. You're safe here now."

"Are they the ones who have Dad?"

"We're not sure, but I don't think so. There's something going on that's a lot bigger than Margo. Like I said before, your parents have been working to crack a whole network of bear abuse. It's more likely that whoever's at the top is who has your dad." He paused, then said, "I know it's a lot to take in, Spence. And I can answer any questions you want, but I think it's time we got some rest. For tonight, we're safe, your parents are both okay, and we've got a really strong team working on getting them home ASAP."

Spencer still had questions, but he was struggling to keep his eyes open. As long as he knew Mom and Dad were going to be okay, he could wait to hear the rest tomorrow.

"Where's your room?" he asked. He felt a little better, but he wasn't sure he wanted to sleep in here alone.

"My room's down the hall," a new voice chimed in. Uncle Mark and Spencer both looked to the door in surprise. A chestnut-colored snout was poking into the room.

Kate pushed her head in farther and looked at Spencer. "Wanna see?"

"Oh . . . um . . ." He was way too tired for another tour.

"Spencer was just about to go to bed, Kate," Uncle Mark jumped in. "Do you want me to stay in here with you, Spence?"

"Do you want *me* to stay in here with you?" Kate said, putting one paw in front of the other as slowly as possible, as though they might not notice, until she was completely in the room.

"Kate Dora Weaver!" Bunny's voice called from the hallway. The cub's ears twitched, but she didn't move to go.

"Kate, I think your—" Before Uncle Mark could finish his sentence, a large paw reached into the room and gently pulled Kate back out into the hallway. The door clicked shut behind her.

16

Spencer woke in his bunk bed and stretched. Evarita usually only made pancakes on weekends, but maybe he could convince her to make an exception. He was starving. He moved to sit up, ready to call to her, but every muscle in his body protested. Yesterday's events came rushing back. Evarita couldn't make him pancakes this morning, and no matter how much it looked like it, this wasn't really Spencer's bedroom. He was in Bearhaven. His aching legs confirmed it.

Poking his head over the side of the top bunk, Spencer looked down to see if his uncle was still in the bottom bunk. Uncle Mark had stayed last night, despite the fact that his feet stuck out over the end of the bed. It had taken every bit of energy Spencer had left to climb the ladder and get into bed himself. He'd practically been asleep before he made it to the top bunk. Now he felt like he had slept for days.

Uncle Mark wasn't in bed. He was probably having breakfast. The thought made Spencer's stomach growl. He'd never finished that peanut butter sandwich . . . Sitting up, he rolled himself out from under his blue-and-silver comforter. He clambered onto the ladder, made his bed, and jumped down, landing unevenly on something much too soft to be the floor.

"GRAHH!" a roar filled the room.

"AHHHH!" Spencer screamed and leaped onto the bottom bunk. He peered over the edge to find the black, leathery pad of a chestnut-colored paw poking out from underneath the bed. It wiggled around and was soon joined by a second paw, and before long, Kate had squirmed out on her belly.

"You stepped on me!"

"I didn't know you were there!" Spencer answered, relieved that it was only Kate. How had she gotten here? He was sure that Bunny had taken her back to her own room last night. Kate sat brushing herself off.

"I slept here," she answered. "It's really like three beds. One—" She pointed to the top bunk. "Two—" She pointed to the lower bunk. "Three—" She motioned to the floor. "Mom said you might be sad, so I came back to keep you company." She shrugged.

"I can't believe you fit under there!" Spencer looked under the bed.

"I liked it. It's like a den. It was like being in the wild." *If the wild was carpeted,* Spencer thought, and then wondered if Kate had ever actually been in the wild. But that didn't seem like the sort of thing you should ask a bear, like asking a new kid on the baseball team if they'd ever seen a bat before.

"Have you seen Uncle Mark?" he asked instead. His stomach growled again, and Kate's ears gave a small twitch.

"No. I've been *sleeping.*" She cocked her head toward the door and sniffed hard. "He's not here. I'd smell him. C'mon!

Mom always leaves breakfast." Spencer looked down at the clothes he'd slept in.

"I need to change."

Kate followed him to the dresser, poking her head into the drawer when he opened it. "What do you need all these clothes for?" She nuzzled and pushed things around. "They all look the same." Spencer reached around the bear to pull out a pair of jeans and a green T-shirt.

"I don't know." He shrugged. "People wear a lot of clothes." He and Kate stared at each other for a moment. *Was she going to leave so that he could change?* Didn't look like it. "Uh . . . do you mind . . . ?" Kate blinked at him. "Could you wait for me outside?"

"Oh! Sure! But hurry, I'm as hungry as a bear!" She burst out in the series of airy chuffing sounds that Spencer was beginning to recognize as her laugh, and then bounded from the room.

When Spencer stepped into the hallway, he found Kate staring so intently at him that he wondered if she'd taken her eyes off the door for one second since settling outside his room to wait. "Last night, Mom said I could show you around before school. I know *everything* about Bearhaven." She started down the hallway. "I *especially* know all the buildings," she added matter-of-factly. "Mom designs them, you know. And she designs all the homes, too!"

"Really?" Spencer looked around the hallway in surprise. The cub puffed with pride.

With Kate walking on all fours beside him, Spencer could see that her BEAR-COM was fastened around her neck by a wide, stretchy-looking band. Like a necklace, but more secure.

"Can you take that off yourself? Your BEAR-COM?" he asked as they reached the stairs.

"Yeah, but it's not *that* easy, so I can just turn it off, too." That explained why Spencer couldn't understand some of the bears last night. They must have had their BEAR-COMs turned off.

The oversized stairs that had seemed nearly impossible to Spencer last night didn't seem so bad now.

"Why would you want to?"

"I didn't say I did!" Kate answered quickly, before going on. "We're not *really* supposed to . . . Dad says it's a sign of respect—for Bearhaven—to keep your BEAR-COM on. Even without humans around. He says it's an *honor* to have BEAR-COMs at all. He had the first one, you know. He helped *invent* it. Anyway, other bears turn them off, sometimes. If they just want to use Ragayo. But Mom says you have to have a good reason—"

"Ragayo?" They stepped into the Weavers' cavernous living room and kitchen. Nobody was there. Spencer had hoped for more information about his parents. He wanted to get to work on finding them, but with nobody here—

"Ragayo is our language," Kate answered. "All bears speak Ragayo. I could teach you some, maybe. If you promise not to tell Mom that I turned off my BEAR-COM." She stopped walking and stared at Spencer, her head cocked to one side, until he nodded solemnly back at her.

"I promise," he said, questions beginning to pile up.

"Okay, good. Now watch this!" She faced Spencer on her hind legs. Her BEAR-COM glittered pink in the sunlit room, and its green light radiated from the base of her neck.

With one claw, she pressed a red button on the side of the device. When she did, a green button popped out on the other side, and the green light blinked off.

"Graflaui!" No translation followed Kate's grumble and grunt. She huffed out a giggle, then moved her claw to the other side of the BEAR-COM and pushed the green button back in. The red button popped out and the device shone green once more. "See? I said, Let's eat!"

Spencer smiled as the cub trotted over to the kitchen counter. He didn't know if he'd ever get used to bears talking to him, but their technology was awesome, and after seeing Jo-Jo and Winston playing *Salmon King* last night, he was pretty sure that the BEAR-COM wasn't the only cool invention these bears had come up with.

Kate retrieved two bowls, one by one, with her mouth, and set them on the table. "This one's for you," she said, scooting one of the bear-sized bowls toward Spencer. He stepped closer, but didn't bother sitting down. If he sat, there was no way he'd be able to see his breakfast, let alone eat out of the huge basin it came in.

"Uh . . ." he started, looking around for a spoon.

"Don't tell me you don't like berries and honey!" Kate practically shouted as she happily plunged her snout into her breakfast.

Spencer laughed. "No, I love berries and honey." He looked down into his own sticky bowl. How important could table manners be when you were eating with a bear cub? He scooped up a handful of berries, his fingers immediately coated in honey, and scarfed it down.

17

Spencer and Kate stepped out into the bright sunshine, and Bearhaven came into focus.

Last night, everything had felt like a dream, unbelievable and covered in darkness. He'd been afraid, exhausted, and confused, but now, with Kate as his guide, Spencer could see Bearhaven for what it was: a very real town full of way more bears than he'd expected.

"We'll start in the center!" Kate called as she bounded down the path, Spencer following at a jog.

Bustling around them, the bears were as varied in color and age as they were in size. As they passed, Spencer could see that a number of the bears were scarred, some were missing eyes or ears or paws, and others looked as though they were in perfect condition, as healthy and energetic as Kate beside him. In the light of day, any fear that Spencer had about being surrounded by bears melted away. Instead, he was fascinated and determined to learn everything he could.

Kate turned onto one of the larger paths that cut through to the square. Following, Spencer tried to memorize where the Weavers' home was, so that he could get back there later on his own if he had to. He noted that only one other small path intersected this larger one before they came to Raymond's Café. At least he'd be able to find which path they lived on, and then Kate would probably just smell him and fling open the door.

"Hey, Kate," Spencer started, reminded of the design carved into the Weavers' door. "The design on the door of your home—"

"My mom did that! With her claws!" Kate answered before Spencer could finish his question.

"Did she do all of them?" He scanned a row of doorways. Each was crosshatched with claw marks but none of them looked the same.

"Oh, no! She designs the *homes*, and she did our door, but every family does their own door. Ours is the best, though. Ask anyone." Kate turned her attention to the stone building that she'd paused beside. "This is Raymond's. We passed it last night, remember?" Smoke wafted from a chimney, and bears sat around the wooden table in front. "It's our restaurant."

Spencer was still surprised that Bearhaven had a restaurant. After their breakfast of berries, he'd figured that all of the food in Bearhaven was simple and foraged. "What do you get there?" he asked, trying to make out what the bears at the table were eating.

"Salmon nuggets are my favorite! You can try them sometime." Kate dashed off down the path. "Come on!"

Spencer followed. They were circling the square, and between the large stone buildings that stood on its perimeter, there were smaller, brightly colored shops. Kate stopped in the middle of a row of them.

"Food," she said, pointing to a shop with a sign that read *Forage Fresh*. "Lab stuff." She pointed to another shop that seemed to be filled with high-tech gadgets. *Lab stuff?* Before he could ask, Kate dropped to all fours and took off again.

"Kate!" Spencer shouted, running to catch up. This wasn't the tour he'd expected. A race around Bearhaven on sore legs was more than he'd bargained for, even after a long night's sleep, and it wasn't getting him any closer to finding Mom and Dad.

"We haven't even gotten to the good parts, and I have to go to school soon!" She stopped to wait for him. "You want to waste time on the boring stuff?"

"Well, I want to see *every*thing," he said. How was he supposed to know what the boring stuff was?

"Fine. This is Pinky's Rehab Center and Salon," Kate said flatly. Spencer looked at the stone building she was pointing at. It was about the same size as Raymond's, but it had tons of windows with flower boxes hanging from each one. "That's where they help bears when they first get to Bearhaven. Those are the flags. They're *always* up there." Spencer looked up at the flags he'd only barely made out last night, waving over Bearhaven in the darkness. One of the flags was tattered, a dirty green and gold, and looked old. The other flag was black, with the image of a crown resting on an upraised bear claw in shining silver. Kate motioned to another stone building on the square. "That building's called the meetinghouse, but I don't know why. It's not like there are that many meetings. The important ones happen in the Lab anyway. And *those* are secret."

Finally! Something that sounded promising! "What do you mean *secret*?" Spencer tried to sound casual.

"What I mean is that the Bear Council meets in the Lab, and only members are allowed. And nobody is supposed to know when they meet, but *I* do."

"What's the Bear Council?" If anyone was working on getting his parents back, it must be them.

"They're the decision makers in Bearhaven. They oversee everything here, and the rescue missions, too. My mom and dad are on it. Nobody else has *two* parents on the Bear Council. Just me and Jo-Jo and Winston and Aldo and Lisle. Well . . . and you. But you're not a bear, so that's not the same."

"My parents are on the council?" Spencer asked.

"Of *course* your parents are on the council! And your uncle is, too! You're really lucky."

"Do you think they're meeting now?" Spencer asked eagerly. That *had* to be where Uncle Mark and the Weavers were. "Do you think they're making a plan to rescue my parents?"

"Probably," Kate said.

"Where's the Lab?" If they were talking about his parents, Spencer needed to be there. He could help.

Kate huffed. "Well, I've been *trying* to show you that."

"Oh, okay. Let's go, then." Over Kate's shoulder, Spencer could see a group of cubs playing in the square. A cinnamon-colored one broke off and ran toward them.

"Kate!" it called, right before tripping over its own paws and stumbling into Spencer, taking them both down into a heap. "Sorry!"

Spencer tumbled around, trying to extract himself from the tangle of furry limbs. The bear didn't seem to be trying quite as hard to right itself. Instead, Spencer had a feeling that the cub was sniffing him, brushing a clumsy paw across

Spencer's head on purpose. Then the cub's tongue darted out and slurped up Spencer's forearm.

"Hey!" Spencer shouted, half laughing and half grossed out.

"Reggie, you're such a chipmunk!" Kate cried, and leaped into the fray, tackling Reggie and dragging him away from Spencer. "You have to be gentle. Spencer Plain is a *human*."

"Sorry," Reggie said sheepishly. He sat up and fixed his brown eyes on Spencer. "What're you guys doing?"

Spencer brushed himself off. "Taking a tour." He didn't mind being bowled over by the cub; it's not like it hurt. He didn't even mind being *tasted* by the cub, but he definitely didn't want the cub to delay their getting to the Lab.

"Can I come?" Reggie asked.

"If you can keep up!" Kate hollered, and took off at a gallop.

18

Spencer recognized the path as they raced along it. He'd seen it last night. It was the one that connected the center of Bearhaven to the dock at the river's edge.

They passed three intersecting pathways, three rings of bear homes, before the path took them out into the open valley. Trees and bushes extended in either direction, growing thicker as they approached the river. Kate slowed to a walk as they neared the riverside.

The river widened by the dock, creating calmer pools near the shore. Brown and orange fish darted beneath the surface of the crystal-clear water, and toward the middle, twigs and leaves swept by on the steady current.

On the dock, facing away from them, stood a huge, very muscular bear. Kate motioned for them to be quiet as they stepped closer.

"Reach for the vines!" the bear boomed through the massive headset propped between his big, furry ears.

"Fred Crossburger," Reggie whispered to Spencer. "My mom says he gives 'bulking up for winter' a whole new meaning." Kate hushed them again, and then mimed stretching for imaginary vines above her, stifling a giggle.

Taking a step closer, Spencer could see that beyond Fred, standing chest-high in the water, was a group of bears, their paws above their heads. They stretched toward the sky, alternating paws.

"What's wrong, Maisie?" Fred chided one of the bears who'd dropped her paws back into the water. "You don't want those delicious blueberries at the top of the tree?"

Examining the microphone that extended out of Fred's headset, Spencer noticed a fat diamond stud in one of his furry ears, glimmering in the sunshine.

"Blueberries don't grow on trees, Fred," Maisie grumbled. "They grow on bushes."

"Class, you can thank Maisie later," Fred shouted cheerfully into his microphone. "Ten more for being literal!" The bears groaned.

Kate rolled her eyes and ducked through the row of trees beside them. Reggie hopped through behind her, and Spencer followed, stepping onto a small path that he hadn't noticed before. It was different than the others in Bearhaven: unmarked and made of dirt.

Reggie sniffed the air around them. "Hey! This is the way to the—"

"The Lab," Kate finished, grinning.

"But we're not allowed!" Reggie sat back on his haunches. He looked, wide-eyed, from Kate to Spencer.

Not allowed? Spencer was even more sure that he needed to get to the Lab now. "What's this lab all about, anyway?" he said, still walking. Maybe if he could get Reggie talking, the cub would forget they were headed somewhere they weren't supposed to go. Kate kept going, too, falling in beside Spencer as Reggie started to chatter, following behind.

"It's the most high-tech place in Bearhaven! All of the power comes from the Lab, and things are made there. Like the BEAR-COMs and security stuff and everything. Only the Bear Guard and the Bear Council are supposed to go there. Even the bears *training* for the guard aren't allowed near the Lab until they pass the test and get their official cuffs. I'm going to be on the Bear Guard, you know."

"The Bear Guard?" Spencer asked.

"Our security?"

"He doesn't know, Reggie. He just got here," Kate said. "The guard protects Bearhaven," she explained to Spencer, "and keeps Bearhaven hidden. Their headquarters are in the Lab. My brother Aldo just made it through training, so now he gets to go to the Lab and wear the silver cuffs and everything."

So Bearhaven had its own police force. Professor Weaver really must have meant it when he said that they were well equipped to help Mom and Dad.

Kate stopped abruptly, and Reggie, who'd been examining Spencer from head to toe, bumped into her back.

"Hey!" she shouted, then clapped a paw over her BEAR-COM. Their path ended at the edge of a clearing a few feet ahead, and in the clearing sat—

"The Lab . . ." whispered Reggie.

Spencer took a step forward, but Kate gently butted him back.

The Lab didn't look like anything else in Bearhaven. A perfectly round dome, it sat in the center of the clearing and seemed to be constructed out of some sort of pitted metal.

Smooth circular scoops evenly covered the shiny surface of the dome, making it look as if some huge silver golf ball had been nestled into the ground.

"How do you get in?" Spencer asked. He couldn't see any doors or windows.

"It's impossible," Kate said. "Unless you're *supposed* to get in, you can't."

Impossible? But Spencer had to get in there. "Have you ever tried?"

"No way!" Reggie yelped.

Kate jumped. "Did you hear that?"

Spencer hadn't heard anything, but Kate spun around. "The bell!"

"What bell?" Spencer was sure he hadn't heard a bell.

"The school bell!"

"We're going to be late!" Kate and Reggie gasped at the same time, tripping over each other as they scrambled back down the path.

"Come on, Spencer!" Kate called before disappearing around a bend. "Last one there's a hibernator!"

But Spencer didn't follow. He turned back to the Lab.

19

Maybe Kate was right, Spencer thought, discouraged. He'd walked the perimeter of the clearing twice, searching the Lab for any sort of entrance, and found nothing. He'd stolen his way up to the side of the dome and circled it again. But even up close he couldn't find a door or window or hatch anywhere. There wasn't so much as a crack or seam on the whole thing.

Spencer rested his forehead against the dome's cool metal surface. If there wasn't an entrance *on* the Lab, maybe there was an entrance *under* the Lab. Resolving to circle the edge of the clearing again and look for a trapdoor or a hidden tunnel, he took a deep breath and sighed. And then, the metal rippled.

Yes!

Eagerly, Spencer pressed against the curved metal with all of his weight, but nothing happened. He ran his fingers along the surface, prodding it, frantically looking for anything that would allow him access. There was nothing.

"What am I doing wrong?" Spencer muttered. Taking a step back, he examined the spot where he'd felt movement. He *had* felt movement. He knew he had. It had happened right under his forehead . . .

Maybe . . .

Feeling a little silly, he put his forehead in the exact same spot. Nothing happened. He waited. Still nothing.

"Come on," he grumbled. And just for a second, he felt a ripple spread across the cool metal and then vanish, like breath on glass.

Like breath! His breath!

Spencer lifted his head off the dome and positioned his mouth like he was about to take a big bite out of the surface.

"Open sesame!" he proclaimed, then filled his lungs and blew hard onto the Lab. The metal wall shimmered and the dimples smoothed out. The area of the wall he'd breathed on became transparent and then seemed to disappear altogether, leaving a ragged hole about the size of Spencer's head. Through it, Spencer could see what appeared to be an empty lobby with hallways breaking off to both sides.

Spencer cautiously extended his right hand toward the hole, afraid the wall might snap shut like a Venus flytrap and eat his arm.

"What the . . . ?" Spencer jerked his hand back.

Instead of going through the hole, his fingers had been stopped by an invisible film that felt delicate and a little sticky, like a deflated balloon.

Spencer shook out his hand and stretched his fingers. "Okay, I can do this," he whispered, and extended his right hand into the hole more forcefully this time. He pushed harder against the film for a moment, and with a slight popping sound, his hand broke through to the other side. He resisted the urge to stop there and examine whatever crazy technology the bears had developed to make this wall possible, and pushed the rest of his arm through, and then his shoulder. Taking another deep breath, he blew on the wall around the hole, widening the gap until the opening was big enough to fit his entire body.

This is so cool, Spencer thought, before squeezing his eyes shut and plunging through the wall into the room beyond.

As he stumbled to regain his balance, he heard a soft crackling sound and watched as the wall re-formed smoothly behind him. Spencer stood still for a moment. It didn't seem like anyone had heard him break in. "Better not wait and find out," he muttered as it dawned on him that he needed to find someone he knew before a bear that he didn't know found him first.

The broad hallways off the lobby were sleek and white. He started down the left one, staying close to the wall and walking as quietly as he could. The first door he came to was open; Spencer didn't hear anything and cautiously peeked inside.

Just as cavernous and white as the hallway, the room was filled with tables of electronic equipment. Each table was equipped with a robotic arm, and at the end of each robotic arm was a mechanical replica of a human hand. *Creepy.*

Sure that nobody was inside, Spencer stepped into the room to get a closer look. The metal parts and wires spread across the tables reminded him of his computer project, lying untouched and unassembled on his desk at home. *Of course. They need the robotic hands because huge bear paws can't work with such small mechanics.* Maybe Professor Weaver could give him a tour of the Lab later. If he wasn't too mad that Spencer had gotten in on his own.

Poking his head back out into the hallway, Spencer checked for bears, then left the room. As cool as the Lab was, he had to find that Bear Council meeting.

Spencer crept down the hallway, passing a few closed doors before finding another open one. He flattened himself against the wall, and then leaned over just enough to peek inside. Quickly, he pulled back, his pulse racing. The room wasn't empty, and it didn't look anything like the last one.

"Yeah, I've got her on camera two," a voice said. Spencer guessed the speaker was the bear whose back was turned to the door. There was a reply, but Spencer couldn't make out the words: It was fainter, and even more electronic. *He must be using the BEAR-COM like Professor Weaver and B.D. did last night. Like walkie-talkies.* "More fog to the northeast perimeter," the bear said. "Yes, I'm *sure.*"

Spencer leaned in to get another glimpse of the room. He looked beyond the bear to a long, crescent-shaped console lined with oversized computer monitors. His eyes immediately went to the second screen in the row.

The monitor showed a girl in the woods. He thought she might be a little older than him, though not much—but what was she doing?

"Where's that fog?" the bear boomed into his BEAR-COM, making Spencer jump. "She's taking more photographs."

The bear was right. The girl on screen was aiming her phone at the plants and roots at her feet and taking pictures. She reached for the pen that was tucked behind one ear, then suddenly, it got harder for Spencer to see her. Within seconds, the image on the screen was almost totally obscured by silvery fog. *The fog!* The same fog that Spencer had gotten caught in last night. It was being produced by the bears!

"Aldo," said a gruff voice from a part of the room that Spencer couldn't see. He pulled back, pulse racing, and started to slide down the hallway, staying flat against the wall.

"What's going on here?"

"Nothing to worry about. It's definitely Kirby this time. Just sent more—" The answer was cut off by a low growl.

"No. Here."

B.D. stepped into the hallway.

20

"Aldo, have you had the pleasure of meeting Spencer Plain?" B.D. asked as he maneuvered his massive body in a way that left Spencer no choice but to enter the room. Spencer noticed the silver cuffs on B.D.'s front legs. The bear hadn't been wearing them when they'd met in the woods yesterday, and somehow, the cuffs of the Bear Guard made B.D. look even more powerful. Spencer gulped.

"Uh, nice to meet you," he said to Aldo, who was staring at him accusingly. "You're one of the Weavers, right?"

"He is also new to the guard," B.D. said gruffly. "Obviously. Since yesterday he so skillfully sent fog down on both of us, and today he chose to focus on a child miles away in the woods, rather than the one right here, who broke in under his nose."

Aldo mumbled an apology and cast a dejected glance back at the fogged screen of camera two.

"Who is that girl?" The moment he'd asked, Spencer regretted it. Apparently B.D. didn't think he was in a position to be asking anything.

"I don't make a habit of sharing security concerns with trespassers," B.D. answered tersely. "We can discuss how you got into this facility later. It seems you are smarter and more persistent than I would have given you credit for, but at the moment I have more important things to do than hear about your little game of hide-and-go-hunt in the Lab."

"It's not a *game*!" Spencer's voice was louder than he'd intended. "I came to see the council!"

B.D. and Aldo stared at him, then Aldo swiveled around to face the bank of computers. *Uh-oh.*

"I beg your pardon?" B.D. said slowly, quietly.

"I have to talk to the Bear Council," Spencer said more calmly. "I know they're meeting here." B.D.'s eyes bore down on him. He wanted to run, but he stood his ground. Mom and Dad needed help. His help. "B.D., please? It's my family they're talking about. I have to help find my family." For a second, Spencer thought he saw a glimmer of sympathy in the bear's eyes, but then it was gone.

"I'm sorry, Spencer, but council meetings are closed. I'm sure you will be given information about your parents shortly. Aldo will show you to the exit." At the sound of his name, Aldo jumped to attention. B.D. lumbered over to one side of the room and stepped onto a large silver slab on the floor. He hit a white button that blended into the wall behind him. The slab, which Spencer saw now was really a platform, lowered B.D. quickly into the ground with a soft hydraulic *whooosh*.

It was the same as the platform in the tree last night. The council must be meeting underground, beneath the Lab. A moment passed and the silver platform reappeared, without B.D. on top of it, and closed the gap in the floor.

"All right, Spencer," Aldo said, "time to go."

I've got to get down there.

"I'm sorry for getting you in trouble, Aldo," Spencer said, turning to the bear whose job it was to keep him from doing what he planned to. Distracting Aldo was his only chance.

"It's okay," Aldo answered. His demeanor had changed. B.D. might not have been swayed by Spencer's plea to help his family, but Aldo looked much more sympathetic . . . He was Bunny's son after all. "It was my fault, really. Silly mistake. I smelled you, but I was watching Kirby on the screen. Should've known that human stink was way too strong to be coming from her out there."

"So that girl—Kirby?—she's taking pictures and trying to get into Bearhaven?" Spencer walked over to the bank of computer screens. There were a dozen of the oversized monitors, each numbered with a metal plate at the top, and from the control panel below it looked like the Bear Guard could change the angle of each camera. *They must be able to survey every inch of the perimeter from in here . . .*

"It's hard to say," Aldo said, sitting down at the console again. "Kirby's been poking around for a while now. She's definitely looking for something, but we don't think she knows exactly what she's looking for." The bear shrugged, tapped some buttons on his oversized keypad, and looked beyond Spencer to scan the security screens. "B.D. thinks it's important to take all activity close to the perimeter of Bearhaven seriously, though."

The fog that the bears had manufactured to engulf Kirby was fading, and through the misty feed of camera two, Spencer could tell that the girl was gone now. He was disappointed not to get another glimpse of her. She would know how he'd felt . . . out there alone in that thick fog. Had it made her think the same things he had—all of a sudden needing to go home?

"So *you* sent it?" Spencer suddenly asked, remembering what B.D. had said. "The fog?"

"Yeah, sorry about that . . . It was a mistake. B.D.'s not too happy with me about it." The bear glanced down at his silver cuffs.

Spencer scanned the screens, but didn't find Kirby anywhere. The Bear Guard's fog must have worked, sending her back to wherever she'd come from.

"How'd you get in here anyway?" Aldo asked, heading toward the door and motioning Spencer to follow.

"I sort of just, uh . . . breathed on the wall?" Spencer looked back at Aldo sheepishly but didn't move toward the door. "It was an accident, I guess."

Aldo rose on his hind legs, his silver cuffs flashing, and Spencer tensed, but instead of towering over Spencer to reprimand him, the bear leaned up against the door frame and slid up and down and back and forth, scratching his back.

"I guess that would make sense," Aldo said once he'd finished scratching and dropped back to all fours, a thoughtful look on his face. "We breathe in, too. It's the skin of the building—that special metal that covers the structure, you know? It has sensors that detect DNA—" The bear suddenly stopped talking and looked anxiously toward the platform that had carried B.D. underground. "There's no way I'm supposed to be telling you all this." He shook his head, clearly unhappy with himself. "We should—"

"Wait! DNA?" The lab's technology was even more advanced than Spencer had imagined. "The wall of the Lab knows my *DNA*?"

"Not yours, little man. Your parents have access, and your uncle Mark. Same thing happened with me. They didn't have to program me in when I got onto the guard, because my parents already had access." Aldo stepped up to Spencer. "That's top secret," he said seriously, his breath hot in Spencer's face. "You can't tell anyone that. I could lose my—"

"No, no . . . of course not!" Spencer sputtered. "I won't, Aldo, I promise."

"I never should have said anything," the bear reprimanded himself. "I'm still getting used to all these rules." He looked at the silver cuffs on his wrists and then shook his head rigorously, like he was shaking off the mistake. "You heard the boss. Time to get you out of here." Aldo turned back to the door.

"There she is again! It's Kirby!" Spencer shouted suddenly, pointing to the computer screens. Aldo rushed over and pushed Spencer aside as he sat at the console.

"Where?" he asked, a claw poised above his BEAR-COM, ready to radio.

"Camera four," Spencer answered quickly. They looked at camera four's monitor. Aside from trees and a few clusters of large rocks, there was nothing there. "I *just* saw her, I swear," Spencer insisted. "She must've jumped behind the rocks!"

Aldo leaned forward to search the screen, grunting a string of untranslated Ragayo that Spencer took for cursing. Spencer began to back away.

"She couldn't have seen the camera . . ." Aldo muttered, adjusting the camera's angle, trying to get a better picture of the rocks.

Now!

Spencer sprinted toward the silver platform, slamming his hand against the white button camouflaged on the wall. The platform instantly began to lower. Aldo growled in protest and bounded across the room, skidding to a halt at the edge of the opening to the fast-dropping platform. He tried to scoop Spencer up, but Spencer flopped to his belly and lay just out of reach.

21

Spencer rolled off the platform as soon as it stopped, and bounded to his feet. He was in a hallway identical to the ones aboveground, sleek and white, except this one had only one door, a great wooden one, at the very end of the passage.

He took off running. B.D. could appear to take him away any moment, and he didn't know how Aldo might try to stop him.

If I could just get into that room, I could convince them . . .

He was almost to the door when it swung open and B.D. stepped out to block his way. Spencer skidded to a halt, facing the enormous bear, and searched for a way he might dodge past him. "Council meetings are *closed,* Spencer. I understand you want to help your family, but I'm afraid that I still cannot—"

Before Spencer could make his best attempt at getting by, Bunny Weaver appeared and slipped in beside B.D. Spencer looked up at her pleadingly. *Please understand.*

"Perhaps we can make an exception this once, B.D.," she said, patting the larger bear's forearm. "He's gotten this far. We can at least speak to the boy." Spencer held his breath, waiting for B.D.'s reply.

After what seemed like forever, B.D. nodded, as though relieved not to be responsible for keeping Spencer out or letting him in. He shrugged and turned back into the room.

"This way, Spencer," Bunny said warmly, and led him through the ominous door.

Clutching the jade bear in his pocket, Spencer entered the council room. He expected a room as forbidding as the door that led to it, or as sterile as the Lab, but instead he found himself in a cozy room. It looked like a bear's den, or at least what he imagined a souped-up bear's den might look like. A long wooden table heaped with huge mugs and bowls of food stretched through the middle of the room. On either side, broad couches, high-backed armchairs, and wide, cushioned seats flanked the table, bears filling every one. Well, almost every one.

Uncle Mark sat by himself on a plush-looking couch, space for two other people, or one other bear, empty beside him. *Mom and Dad must sit there,* Spencer thought, and removed his hand from the jade bear, his confidence returning.

If not for the wall at the opposite end of the room, Spencer would have had no idea that he was anywhere more official than the Weavers' house. A bank of huge monitors covered the wall. Some displayed maps, others showed surveillance video feeds like the ones Aldo manned upstairs. A few showed messages, or lists of information, and on the screen at the center, straight across the room from Spencer, as though staring him down, was the image of a woman's face.

Goose bumps rose on his arms, and the back of his neck prickled. *Who is she?* Her expression was stony, her muddy brown eyes cold and ringed in dark circles, making her look hollowed out. Her hair hung straggly and thin around her bony face, blond, but greenish, too, as if her own hair was nauseated from having to be attached to such a creepy-looking person.

"Spence!" Uncle Mark called his attention back to the council. Bunny and B.D. had returned to their seats, and Spencer stood at the head of the table. He scanned the faces staring back at him. There was Professor Weaver, Bunny, B.D., a few bears he didn't recognize, and then Yude. As their eyes met, Yude sat forward in his seat, placing his claws firmly on the table in front of him, the green cloak hiding the rest of his body. Spencer tried not to shudder, but there was something about the way Yude looked at him . . .

"He shouldn't be here," Yude snarled, eyes still locked on Spencer. His snarl turned into a thundering growl. "B.D., this is unaccept—"

"*I* allowed Spencer in, Yude, not B.D.," Bunny interrupted, her tone sweet but authoritative. "Though I feel certain that if we were to vote, the majority would allow him to stay long enough to speak his mind."

"He's a child—and he's a Plain," Yude spit in response, but it seemed to be the last he'd say on the matter. He sank back into his chair, allowing the hood of his cloak to fall forward, covering most of his face.

"Spencer, I don't believe you know all of the council members." Professor Weaver took control of the situation. "This is Raymond, our culinary expert and the chef behind Raymond's Café," he began casually, and Spencer felt the tension ease a little around him. A bear wearing a bandanna around his neck and a chef's hat the size of a fire hydrant raised a paw to salute Spencer.

"This is Pinky," Professor Weaver continued, interrupting a bear as she reached for a bowl of grapes. Her claws were painted electric pink. "She runs the rehab center."

"And salon," Pinky added, waggling her shockingly bright claws at Spencer. "I like to say we help our bears inside and out."

Professor Weaver continued around the table, introducing Mr. Bee, the school principal, who eyed Spencer appraisingly, and Dr. Dominica Fraser, Bearhaven's dentist, who nodded politely.

Professor Weaver gestured to an older-looking bear sitting in a plush chair beside Uncle Mark. She chimed in before the professor could say anything. "Saving the best for last, I see," she said, smoothing the rust-colored blanket on her lap. "I'm Grandmama Grizabelle, dear. Now come take a seat and tell us what it is you have to say."

Pleased to have identified the bear as older than the others just by looking at her large but unmuscled size and the thinning fur around her eyes and muzzle, Spencer dropped down beside Uncle Mark. He didn't want to give anyone else a chance to protest his being there, particularly because he wasn't sure whose side Uncle Mark was on.

"I'm here to find out what's happening with my parents. I want to help find them," he blurted out, and then looked into each bear's eyes, trying to make the council see his determination.

Yude switched off his BEAR-COM. *"Ig ha ru afanval-yar!"* He spewed a steady stream of angry-sounding grunts and snorts into the room.

22

Grandmama Grizabelle spoke over the squabbling that had erupted in the council room. "As members of this council, we are united under all circumstances. *Plain*"—she put a sharp emphasis on the word—"and simple. Now, let's all get ahold of ourselves." With pursed lips and a stern look, she scanned the room, challenging anyone there to continue the debate that Yude had begun in Ragayo. Spencer didn't need to know what Yude had said to know that the bear didn't want him there. Luckily, the matter seemed to have been settled.

At least that's over. Spencer let out a loud sigh of relief, and at the sound, everyone turned to stare at him. *Oops.*

"As for you, young man," Grandmama Grizabelle went on. "You're absolutely right that this concerns you." She sat back in her chair, satisfied with her decree, and waited for someone else to step in. Spencer was glad to see that it was Professor Weaver who took charge again.

"All right, Spencer, you may stay as long as the conversation relates to your parents and their safety," he said sternly. "However, everything that you hear in this room must remain in this room, do you understand?"

Yude huffed as he switched his BEAR-COM back on, and Uncle Mark shot him a warning glare. Spencer didn't know why Yude was so angry with him—or his parents.

"Yes, I understand," Spencer answered, resisting the urge to launch into his string of questions. From what he could tell, he was only barely being allowed to stay. Demanding a bunch of information all at once might not be the best way to start.

"Good. Now, B.D. is the Head of the Bear Guard. He'll bring you up to speed." Professor Weaver turned to B.D. *Head of the Bear Guard? No wonder B.D. takes everything so seriously . . .*

With a nod, B.D. went to the wall of monitors, pointing to a large map. "Jane and Shane—your parents—were on a bear rescue mission in Stantonville at the time of your father's capture. The last communication we received from your mother was sent from a location a little farther south, but as you know, she wasn't able to tell us where your father was being taken."

Spencer couldn't stop himself from asking, "Is that who took my dad?" He pointed to the creepy woman whose face was still displayed at the center of the wall.

"We don't believe so, no," B.D. answered.

"That's Margo Lalicki, Spence," Uncle Mark spoke up. "I told you about her last night, remember?"

"The bear handler from Gutler University? The one in the Corvette with the football giant?" Spencer stared back at the woman on the screen. Uncle Mark had said that Margo Lalicki didn't have a good bone in her body, but he didn't know she'd look so . . . scary.

"Yes," Uncle Mark continued. "Your parents have been investigating her for years now. They'd hoped that the mission in Stantonville might lead them to whoever Margo and Ivan work for."

"The people behind the network of bear abuse," Spencer added.

"That's right," confirmed Professor Weaver.

Mr. Bee cleared his throat. "To explain," he began formally, straightening the blue-and-silver-striped tie around his neck. *Definitely a principal.* "At the top of this 'network of bear abuse,' someone is implanting bears with microchips. Once implanted, the bears can be controlled physically, and, we suspect, mentally. Shane and Jane—pardon me, *your parents*—have made progress toward uncovering exactly who is behind the microchipping. At the time of your father's capture, they were working to understand the motivation and technology behind the control."

"We believe that your parents may have gotten much closer while on this latest mission," B.D. added.

"So the boss has my dad?" He'd come to the council hoping for good news and a rescue plan. This was sounding worse by the second. *Microchipped bears?*

"As of now, we think so." B.D. moved to a different screen, where a picture of an adult bear and two cubs was displayed.

"But what does *she* have to do with it?" Spencer pointed back at Margo.

"About to get there, Spence." Uncle Mark put a hand on Spencer's shoulder reassuringly.

"This is Ro Ro Rubin and her cubs." B.D. nodded to the bears on the screen. "About a month ago, Ro Ro decided that she and her family would leave Bearhaven to return to the wild—"

"They lived here and they decided to leave? But why?" Spencer remembered what Uncle Mark had said about some bears being rehabilitated and then returning to the wild, but after seeing how comfortable Bearhaven was and how safe it seemed, he couldn't imagine why a bear would ever want to leave.

"This life isn't for every bear." Bunny sounded sad. "It can feel too . . . overwhelming for some."

"Too *human*, you mean," Yude said sourly.

Bunny ignored him. "Margo Lalicki managed to snatch Ro Ro almost as soon as she left Bearhaven."

"And the little ones, too." Pinky shook her head. "Terrible."

B.D. continued, "We believe Margo sold Ro Ro and her cubs to a man named Jay Grady for his weekly bear-baying show at Grady's Grandstand in Stantonville. He pays a lot for bears, and we've had a hard time closing in on him. Your parents' mission was to rescue Ro Ro and her cubs from Grady's Grandstand, and search for more leads on Margo and her brother and whoever they're working for."

"What's bear baying?"

"Oh, it's just barbaric!" Pinky growled, throwing her electric pink–clawed paws up in the air.

"It is cruel. Bear abuse," Bunny said, shuddering.

"Ladies," Grandmama Grizabelle broke in, "let's give the boy some information."

"Allow me," Mr. Bee said. "Essentially, bear baying is a forced fight in which a bear is chained down while hunting dogs attack. The bear defends itself, hurting the dogs in turn. It's an ugly scene from start to finish." The principal paused, seeming to steel himself for what he had to say next. "Along with being chained, the bears are often defanged and declawed, so that they are defenseless. The bears suffer incredible pain when their teeth and claws are removed, and then there are the wounds they suffer from the dogs during the bear baying. The psychological toll is also extensive." Mr. Bee shook his head, then smoothed out his tie with one great paw and continued. "Spencer, bear baying is a practice that dates back hundreds of years, and even though it is illegal in most places, there are communities across this country that have kept it around."

Spencer felt sick. "But why? Why would anyone do something like that to a bear?" Spencer looked at the bears around him, trying to imagine someone who would want to treat any of them so horribly.

"For entertainment and for money," Uncle Mark answered gravely. "Greedy people know that crowds will come to watch the fight. It's criminal."

"So that's what's happening to Ro Ro? And the cubs? How will the cubs survive that?" Spencer looked to B.D. If Mom and Dad hadn't made it back from the mission, Ro Ro and her cubs must still be there . . .

"It's not likely that Grady would involve the cubs in the baying," B.D. said, "but unfortunately, your parents weren't able to get any of them out before your dad was captured. Ro Ro will be in the show Monday evening; that only gives us forty-eight hours to prepare and a day to travel."

"We have to get to her first," Uncle Mark finished.

"And Mom and Dad?"

Uncle Mark looked to B.D., who motioned for him to go on. "Rescuing your parents is obviously a top priority, but I promise you, your mom and dad are also working to get themselves out of whatever trouble they're in. They've been doing this a long time, Spence. They'll be okay. We can't say the same for Ro Ro. Rescuing her and her cubs has to come first." Uncle Mark continued calmly, holding up a hand to urge Spencer to wait before protesting. "That said, Grady's Grandstand was the last place we know your parents were. We're going in to save Ro Ro and the cubs, but while we're on the premises, we hope to find clues that can lead us to your parents."

"Great." *Finally, a plan.* "When do we leave?" Spencer's question hung in the air.

A flurry of looks were exchanged across the table, and before anyone could answer, Spencer knew. *They don't think I'm going.*

23

Spencer stomped down the dirt trail to the riverbank. He didn't care if Uncle Mark and the Weavers had promised Mom and Dad that they would keep him safe. He was *going* on that mission.

He wished the council had kept up their habit of disagreeing when it came to him. Instead, as soon as the silence had broken, everyone had clamored to give a reason why he shouldn't be allowed to help with the rescue.

"It's much too dangerous," Bunny had said.

"You're not trained," Uncle Mark had added.

The list continued:

"Your parents want you safe in Bearhaven."

"We're not even certain what we're up against."

"You're just a child."

And on and on, until even Mr. Bee had said his piece. "You should be starting your studies here. There will be quite a bit of catching up to do, particularly in the Fish and Forestry courses."

No way! He wasn't about to stay in Bearhaven to learn about fish and forests while Uncle Mark and B.D. went out to find *his* mom and dad and help the bears that *his* parents were trying to save.

Spencer knew he could help. He was smaller and lighter than Uncle Mark, so he could hide and fit into tight spaces, and he was good with computers and gadgets. True, he was a kid, but nobody would notice a kid! He could do and see and hear things that Uncle Mark couldn't.

He reached the river. Fred Crossburger and his exercise class were gone. He had the dock to himself. He walked out to the end and sat down to think. It seemed like every other week Mom and Dad were away somewhere, busy with something he didn't know much about. But the way he missed them now was different. Before, if he asked when they'd be home, the answer had always been "just a few more days," and in a few more days they'd be there. Now, he couldn't even ask.

Sitting in the council room, hearing about the disgusting bear baying, Spencer had really understood why Mom and Dad did what they did. He'd felt the ferocious anger that he figured they must feel every time they heard about a bear being abused, and he'd felt the determination to do something about it. The council *had* to let him help finish the rescue mission that Mom and Dad had started.

"I'm a kid, but I'm also a Plain," Spencer said aloud. "And the Plains rescue bears."

"Who are you talking to?"

Kate! If she could help change Professor Weaver's mind, maybe he'd have a shot!

Kate was standing on the grass at the head of the dock, looking around and sniffing.

"Oh, nobody," he answered.

Kate bounded down the dock, causing it to wobble and sway under them. Lowering onto her belly, she stretched out beside Spencer, her head poking over the dock's edge, snout close to the surface of the water.

"Why didn't you come to school with Reggie and me this morning?" Kate's eyes followed the fish in the river. "Have you been here all day?"

"No." Spencer shrugged. He wanted to tell Kate all about the Lab and the council meeting, but he wasn't sure yet if she could keep a secret. Still, he needed her help.

"Then where did you—"

"I got into the Lab!" he blurted out. "You were right, the Bear Council was meeting about my parents."

"Really? But how?" Kate scrambled to sit up. "You *saw* the Bear Council? Their meetings are *always top secret*!"

"It's a long story," Spencer said, borrowing a line he felt he'd been hearing a lot lately. "And you *can't* tell anyone. Not even Reggie. But I got into the council meeting. Uncle Mark and B.D. are leaving on a mission in two days to rescue Ro Ro and her cubs, and they're going to look for more information about my parents. I *have* to go with them."

"But the council—"

"The council doesn't want me to go. But I'm going."

"But . . . it's so dangerous," Kate whispered.

"That's what *they* said!"

Kate frowned and slid back onto her belly to watch the fish again.

Spencer hadn't meant to snap at Kate like that. "I know it's dangerous," he said more calmly. "But I can't just sit here worrying about my family. I have to do something." Kate ignored him. "There are bears that need help," he went on. "At least I can help rescue Ro Ro and her cubs, and maybe I'll find some clues that could get my parents back . . ." Kate made no move to respond. "Come on, Kate, you have to help me."

"Help you?" Kate finally answered, but kept her face turned to the river. "What can *I* do? I'm not going. No. Way."

"You don't have to leave Bearhaven. Just help me convince your dad that I should go." If Professor Weaver changed his mind, then the council would come around, Spencer was sure of it.

Kate lifted her head to consider Spencer. "But I don't think you should go," she said quietly. "It's scary out there, Spencer. Rescues are for grown-ups, and if the Bear Council doesn't think you should go—"

"I'm going."

Kate snapped her mouth shut and splashed a paw into the river unhappily. "I'll teach you *Salmon King* if you stay." She pouted.

"Kate—?"

The cub huffed. "Okay, okay!" She wiped droplets of river water off her claws and onto her fur. Spencer waited, afraid to say anything that might change her mind. Once Kate had dried each of her claws, she looked back up at Spencer, her eyes gleaming. "Talking to my dad's never going to work. Talking is what Bear Council meetings are for. It's time for *showing*." Spencer was lost. *Showing what?* "You have to *prove* to them that you should go. That you *can* go."

"How?"

"We have to *train* you for the mission!" Kate answered excitedly. "I'll help you! Then, we'll show them that they *need* your help. You'll be so well trained, they won't be able to say no."

"Okay, let's do it! Do you know what—?"

"Hello, you two!"

They spun around to see Bunny and Professor Weaver emerging from the trees. They looked like they were just out for a stroll, but Spencer guessed the council meeting must have ended and they were coming from the Lab.

Spencer and Kate exchanged a sideways glance. *Had the Weavers heard them planning?*

"Hi, Mom! Hi, Dad!" Kate sang.

"Don't be late for dinner!" Bunny called as she and Professor Weaver turned onto the path that led back to the center of Bearhaven. Spencer waved, and in a moment the bears had rounded another bend in the path.

"That was close!" Kate gasped as soon as her parents were out of earshot. "Okay, are you ready?"

"Ready?"

"Ready to start training, of course!" the cub rushed on. "I'm done with school for today, and tomorrow is Saturday, so we can train then, too, and tonight we have dinner with everyone, so we can—"

Spencer gulped. "Everyone?" He imagined all of Bearhaven's bears gathering hungrily around him at dinnertime . . . "The rest of the family," Kate exclaimed. "It's perfect! Aldo will be there, and Fitch, and my dad!" Spencer wasn't sure what Kate was getting at. Kate saw his confusion and went on in an exasperated tone, "Aldo's on the Bear Guard. Fitch helps my dad in the Lab, and *both* of my parents are on the Bear Council. If we're sneaky, we can figure out exactly what we need to train you to *do*."

"We can do it," he said confidently. "It's the best shot I have."

24

Spencer and Kate stood at the edge of the school yard. They'd crept around the side of the stone school building as quietly as they could, hoping not to run into any other cubs or teachers, only to find that they were completely alone. *I guess bear school and human school aren't so different after all,* Spencer thought. *When the weekend comes, everyone gets out as quickly as possible.*

Kate turned to face Spencer, surprising him with her seriousness. "Reggie says that whoever's best at Bear Stealth in school *always* makes it onto the Bear Guard," she explained. "All the cubs in Bearhaven go through Bear Stealth, because we don't learn it in the wild like other bears."

Spencer surveyed the bears' version of a school yard. It was the size of a football field, and rather than a swing set, basketball hoops, and benches, it had boulders, logs, and other natural obstacles. A row of bushes bordered the yard, and behind it, there was a row of different kinds of trees.

"Okay, so now what?" Spencer asked. "I mean, what *is* Bear Stealth? What do you do out here?"

"Oh! It's hiding!" Kate exclaimed. "Well, hiding, silent walking, moving around secretly. That kind of thing. It's so we can move around the woods safely if we have to. I'll show you!" The cub bounded into the yard and ducked behind a boulder. Spencer kept his eyes on the boulder, waiting for the cub to reappear. A few moments later, he thought he heard a faint rustling from one side of the school yard. He turned just in time to see Kate leap out from beneath the needled limbs of a pine tree. She landed happily on all fours, obviously proud of her performance.

"That was awesome!" Spencer called, impressed by Kate's ability to move around the school yard without him even realizing that she'd left her hiding spot behind the boulder. "Can I try?" he asked, confident that he could do just as good a job as the cub. After all, he was smaller and more agile.

Kate bounded back to Spencer. "Sure," she panted. "Start at the boulder. I'll stay here for a few minutes, then I'll come find you. The longer it takes me to find you, the better you are at Bear Stealth, so don't let me see you!"

Spencer jogged over to the boulder. He ducked behind it and looked around. He examined the boulder itself. Kate was on the other side of it, but several yards away. He turned to look at the trees directly behind him. *If I move back in a perfectly straight line . . .* Picking the tree that looked to be centered behind the boulder, Spencer crouched down and ran straight at it. When he reached the row of bushes that marked the back perimeter of the school yard, he leaped over and slid down onto his back, allowing the row of bushes to hide him.

"Okay, now what?" Spencer whispered to himself. He looked at the oak tree looming above him. It was the one he'd aimed for, but he wasn't about to climb it. Quietly, he rolled onto his belly, and, careful to stay low to the ground, he used his elbows and toes to propel himself around to the other side of the tree that faced away from where Kate was standing.

Perfect! The oak's trunk was split and mostly hollow. A knothole looked like it had rotted out, leaving a gap just big enough for Spencer to slip through. Pushing aside the thought of spiders and other creepy-crawly creatures, he stood up and slid sideways through the crack in the trunk. *This is definitely* not *one of the Bearhaven elevators.*

There was barely enough room for Spencer's entire body inside of the tree, and every breath he took came with the strong smell of wet wood. Something crept along the back of his neck. Spencer shuddered.

"Here I come!" Kate called. A minute passed, and then another. Spencer stood completely still. Soon, there was a rustling sound nearby.

"I can smell you but I can't see you!" the cub sang. Her footsteps circled the tree, then the trunk started to shake, and a little shower of sawdust and wood fell on Spencer's head. *She's climbing the tree . . .* Spencer realized. *Thump.* The tree stopped shaking, and Kate's footsteps circled the tree again.

"Spencer?" Spencer could hear the cub sniffing loudly. "Spencer, where are you?" Suddenly, Kate's snout poked through the crack in the trunk. "*There* you are!" she shouted, extracting her snout. "I didn't even *look* for you in there!" She stepped back, leaving Spencer enough space to wiggle out of the gap in the oak's trunk. He brushed himself off. The bugs

and rotten tree insides were worth it. He was a Bear Stealth master!

"You did great!" Kate exclaimed. "A bear would never be able to get in there!"

Spencer smiled. "Thanks. What's next?"

"Dinner! We have to go, or we're going to be late! But follow me; we can keep training on the way back!" Kate dashed along the row of bushes and turned to head down the side of the school yard toward home. She skidded to a halt and waited for Spencer. "Okay, what do you see?" she asked, motioning to the ground in front of them. Between the row of bushes and the row of trees, the ground was covered with twigs and leaves. It looked completely different from the bare ground Spencer had slid onto a few minutes earlier.

"A bunch of twigs?"

"A *loud* zone," Kate corrected matter-of-factly. "You have to practice your silent walking." Gingerly, Kate stepped onto the bed of twigs and leaves, then carefully started to walk. *Chh, chh, chh.* The sound of the brush under her feet was much quieter than Spencer expected, but he could still hear it. Determined to be completely silent, he set out after her.

CRUNCH CRUNCH CRUNCH!

"I said *silent* walking, not noisy marching!" Kate giggled. "Use all of your muscles. Silent walking isn't just about feet; it's about the whole body." The cub continued, her quiet *chh, chh* picking back up.

Crunch. "Dangit!" Spencer exclaimed. This was harder than it looked.

"Pretend you're as light as a fish bone! Pretend there's a vine pulling you up into the air and carrying you across the ground so that your feet hardly touch."

Spencer tensed his abs and lifted his leg off the ground, trying to think about all of the muscles in his body working at once and lifting upward. He set his foot down. *Chh.* He did it again. *Chh.* "I'm doing it!" *Chh, chh, chh. Crunch.* Slowly, they continued forward until the quiet *chh* sound of their feet was all they could hear, and even that got quieter as they went. When they reached the end of the loud zone, Kate took off, loping toward home.

"Come on!" she cried. "Last one there's a rotten tree trunk!"

When Kate and Spencer burst into the Weavers' home, out of breath and covered in dirt, they found Bunny bustling around the kitchen.

"There you are!" She turned to greet them, and her warm smile immediately faded. Bunny had the same look of surprised dismay that Evarita had every time Spencer handed over his grass-stained baseball uniform to her. "Heavens! What have you two been doing?" After a moment, when neither Spencer nor Kate offered an answer, Bunny continued. "No matter. Go wash up so you can set the table."

Kate dashed out of the room without protesting, but Spencer hung back. "Is Uncle Mark coming? To dinner?" He looked up at Bunny hopefully. Since stomping out of the council meeting that afternoon, Spencer hadn't seen Uncle Mark. If he came to dinner, maybe Spencer could talk to him about the mission again . . .

"No, dear, just you and the Weavers tonight!" Bunny said cheerfully, turning back to her cooking. "I believe your uncle's at Raymond's with B.D. They usually work out mission details there." Spencer's shoulders slumped. Uncle Mark and B.D. were planning without him. "Now, off you go! Your mother would not approve of me putting food into those filthy hands of yours!"

Spencer shoved his hands in his pockets and retreated to his bedroom to get ready for dinner. Just because he wasn't planning the mission with Uncle Mark and B.D. didn't mean he wasn't going. His training had begun, and he had plans of his own.

25

The Weavers' dining room table looked big enough to land a plane on. Wide, cushioned benches surrounded it, making space for at least twenty bears to sit comfortably, and three gleaming beehive-shaped chandeliers hung above, filling the room with a honey-colored light.

Spencer was relieved that Bunny had handed him only nine huge plates to set on the table. He didn't think he could carry even one more of the enormous disks of polished wood.

The plates clattered when Spencer set them down, and Kate jumped out from under the table at the sound.

"Oops," he said, and looked back at the door to make sure nobody else had heard. "What are you doing under there?" he asked.

She scooted back under the table without answering. A moment later, two extra cushions appeared on one of the benches. "They're for cubs," she explained, and then looked at him pointedly. "And cub-sized humans."

Spencer didn't like the idea of having to sit on extra cushions, even if the table was made for bears. He wasn't a baby.

"Go ahead if you don't believe me," Kate said, waggling a paw at an unbolstered bench. Spencer sat down and Kate hopped up beside him. She reached her neck forward and rested her muzzle on the table. Spencer burst out laughing. Leaning forward, he rested his chin on the polished wood. Only their heads cleared it. *Extra cushions it is.*

Spencer scooted over to settle himself on top of one of the two higher seats that Kate had assembled. His chest and shoulders were now above the surface of the table, and he began to relax, enjoying the feeling that he wasn't quite so out of place in Bearhaven after all.

Just then, Professor Weaver walked into the dining room. "Kate, I believe your mother could use some help in the kitchen." He took a seat at the head of the table.

Kate hopped down and scooted toward the door. "Okay, I'll tell Jo-Jo and Winston," she called over her shoulder.

Professor Weaver chuckled. "I think we both know that's not what I meant."

Kate stopped a few steps from the door.

"I can help, too," Spencer offered. He wanted to get a glimpse at whatever it was they were having for dinner. If it was grubs or something, he'd need to be prepared.

"No, no, that's okay, Spencer. Kate, go on upstairs. Let's not make our guest prepare his own welcome dinner."

Professor Weaver looked at his youngest cub warmly, but even through the BEAR-COM Spencer could tell that the professor meant business. Kate huffed and flounced out of the room.

"Your uncle tells me that you enjoy working with technology," Professor Weaver said, turning back to Spencer and clasping his paws on the table.

"Yeah!" Spencer exclaimed, sounding a bit more enthusiastic than he'd planned. *This is perfect,* he thought, preparing to dig for more information. "I've taken apart this computer for a project at school. I'm supposed to put it back together and give a report on it." He paused. His schoolwork was definitely going to pile up while he was gone; Ramona and Cheng would have to fill him in on a *lot* when he got back. And he'd have a lot to tell them about Bearhaven, too. Cheng would go nuts hearing about the BEAR-COMs . . . He pulled his thoughts back to the computer project and Professor Weaver, who was looking at him with interest. "Anyway, it took way longer than I expected, because I kept getting stuck looking at every detail. I wanted to figure it all out, you know?"

"I *do* know," Professor Weaver answered.

"The BEAR-COMs and everything"—Spencer dropped his voice to a whisper—"the Lab wall and the technology there . . . you *made* all of that?"

Professor Weaver laughed. "Not alone, but yes, I developed the BEAR-COM, and even the lab's security, which apparently we need to adjust." The bear cocked his head and shot Spencer a playfully reprimanding look before continuing. "But the BEAR-COM was before Bearhaven. My mentor and I developed the first version together."

"You lived at Gutler University, right?"

"Yes, after the first Professor Weaver adopted me," the bear replied. "I lost my mother to a bear trap in the forest when I was still a cub, no older than Kate, really. I hadn't had much exposure to humans at that point, but I knew that whoever had created the trap had to have a way to open it once it snapped shut, so in desperation, I figured out the mechanics and released my mother. But she didn't survive, even once I'd gotten her out."

"I'm so sorry," Spencer said quietly. His parents had told him lots of stories about the intelligence of bears. He'd loved the fact that they were known to pick locks at zoos and use rocks as tools in the wild, but he'd never considered how their intelligence could be so much like humans', driven by emotions as real as wanting to save their mother.

"It's all right, son," Professor Weaver said. "It was a very long time ago. I ended up with Professor Weaver, a wonderful mentor, and it all led me here. The professor was doing work in the field at the time and happened upon me. He took me in and raised me as his own. We created the BEAR-COM together, a bit selfishly at first. We thought of ourselves as family, and we wanted to understand each other better, but then we started to realize what the BEAR-COM could do for other bears. If we could communicate, bears and humans that is, perhaps we could avoid so many misunderstandings." Professor Weaver threw his front paws up in the air. "Can you imagine? The number of bears who could be saved if they could just explain . . . Anyway, your parents came to the professor regarding the mascot situation at Gutler. The rest is history, as they say."

Before Spencer could ask a single question, bears started piling into the dining room, surrounding Spencer and Professor Weaver in chatter as they filled the seats and covered the table with loads of food.

26

Aldo plopped down onto the bench beside Spencer. "Pinky might have some glasses at the rehab center that you can borrow," he said. "I hear your eyes aren't so *dependable*." Spencer froze. When he'd lied about spotting Kirby on the surveillance screen to escape Aldo earlier that day, he hadn't realized he'd be having dinner with the bear that night. Aldo started to chuckle. "I'm only kidding, little man." He laughed, seeming to forgive Spencer for the trick. Kate sat on Spencer's other side, also elevated, and took advantage of it by making faces at Jo-Jo and Winston, who sat across the table, a little bit lower without cub cushions.

Beside Jo-Jo and Winston sat Fitch, who introduced himself as Professor Weaver's protégé-turned-son-in-law, an introduction that prompted various comments from the others.

"Pro-té-gé?" Jo-Jo piped up. "Nice try with the fancy talk, Fitch. I thought you were just dad's lowly assistant." Winston jabbed Fitch in the belly, joining in his brother's teasing.

"And unless I missed the wedding, you're nobody's son-in-law yet," the bear with a white heart-shaped patch of fur on her chest chimed in from beside Fitch. She winked at Spencer. "Hi, I'm Lisle," she said. From her size, Spencer assumed that she was around the same age as Aldo, maybe a little older, but while Aldo's fur was black and tan like Professor Weaver's, Lisle's fur was more like Bunny's, silver and glossy.

"Lisle and Fitch are engaged," Kate whispered to Spencer.

"It's not a secret, dear," Bunny said from her seat beside Professor Weaver at the head of the table. She lifted her cup to toast. "It's wonderful to have you with us, Spencer. Welcome."

"Thanks!" Spencer reached for the massive clay mug that one of the Weavers had set in front of him and lifted it with both hands to cheers. He clunked his mug against Aldo's and Kate's, unable to reach anyone else's across the large table, then raised the mug to his mouth to take a sip.

"Mmm . . . best bug blood of the season!" Winston exclaimed just as the liquid hit Spencer's lips. He coughed and sputtered, spraying the drink onto the table. Jo-Jo and Winston let out streams of boisterous chuffs.

"Boys . . ." Professor Weaver warned in a low voice. Lisle shot Spencer a sympathetic look.

"Don't mind them," she said. "It's just spring water."

"Oh. Good!" Spencer blushed and wiped the water off his face. He took a sip to show that he'd recovered.

Aldo leaned a shoulder into Spencer. "Let's get it out of the way now, little man," he said conspiratorially, and then pointed to a platter on the table. "That's not monster larvae, it's honey-covered salmon." Pointing to another, he said, "That's not poison ivy, it's mixed spring greens. And so is that one, and that one, and that one." Now that Aldo mentioned it, Spencer realized most of the platters were heaped with salad. "Oh," Aldo went on, "and in the salad, those aren't dead ants, just regular old nuts."

Spencer stole a glance at Jo-Jo and Winston, who were watching sourly as Aldo ruined their fun.

"And this isn't guts." Kate raised a pitcher filled with something that Spencer could have easily been fooled into thinking was guts. "It's smashed raspberry dressing."

"And this isn't—" Aldo started, pointing to the last unidentified platter.

"Okay, okay!" Lisle broke in. "As appetizing as this little game is, I do actually want to *eat* some of this food."

"Thank you, dear," said Bunny. "Spencer, that last dish is dandelion mash. Dig in, everyone."

Aldo and Kate took turns piling a little of each dish onto Spencer's plate, and he wound up with his plate heaped with food. Not that he minded. He was starving.

The Weavers carefully speared their food with their claws or lifted handfuls into their mouths, but Spencer picked up the fork and knife that had been set out for him. *Mom probably left a spoon, too,* he thought, remembering his messy breakfast. As if reading his mind, Kate eyed the silverware suspiciously. After a moment, she shrugged and motioned for Spencer to start eating. He took a bite, then ate ravenously.

Everything was delicious. The salmon was sweet and crispy. The salad had leaves in it that Spencer had never seen before, but was bursting with flavor, sticky from mouth-puckering raspberry dressing. Even the dandelion mash surprised him, creamy and fragrant. Spencer shoveled the food into his mouth, and then looked up to find that at a table full of bears, he was the only one eating like an animal.

"Don't they feed you humans?" Kate giggled. Spencer gulped down a big bite of salmon.

He smiled sheepishly, then realized that this was his chance to change the direction of the conversation. "Aldo, you just joined the Bear Guard, huh?" he asked.

"Yes, he did, and we're so proud of him." Bunny beamed at her son.

"Cool!" Spencer said. "So what does it take? You know, to make it."

Aldo took a swig of water. "Well, it's pretty tough. You train for a year. Then there's a test, and even after the year of training, not everyone passes."

A year? "What's involved in the—"

"What's on the test?" Kate practically shouted, cutting Spencer off. Spencer almost choked on his salad. *That wasn't very sneaky!*

"Oh, you know, lots of physical stuff. Gotta be strong to be on the guard." Aldo flashed a toothy grin. Jo-Jo and Winston snorted. "Bear Stealth, boulder rolling, tree climbing, that sort of thing," Aldo went on. "Then there's the tech test, to make sure we can run the security systems." He cleared his throat. "Top secret stuff, you know. We're also tested on Bearhaven history. Oh, and Rescue Ragayo."

"Rescue Ragayo?" Spencer squeaked. No wonder bears needed a whole year to learn everything!

"That's right." Fitch answered for Aldo, whose mouth was full. "Many of the bears outside of Bearhaven speak a simple form of Ragayo. During rescue missions, our operatives have to be able to communicate fluently with them, but it takes a bit of training, if you are used to speaking Ragayo in Bearhaven."

"Or if you've never spoken Ragayo before," Professor Weaver added, and smiled at Spencer. "Your parents speak Rescue Ragayo, you know. And Mark."

Oh, great. That means it's definitely required. Spencer and Kate exchanged an uneasy look.

"So your Ragayo isn't the same one other bears speak?" Spencer asked.

"It is and it isn't," said Fitch. "Ragayo is rooted in the sounds that bears make, growls and grunts and so on. Most bears use those growls and grunts in a more basic way than we do because they only need simple words for life in the wild. Here in Bearhaven, though, we've created more words so that we can discuss more complicated things." He motioned to the room around them. "Our language has gotten more complex as our environment has."

"It's similar," Lisle said, "to the way a human toddler can speak compared to the way a human adult can."

"Can I take Spencer to see the fireflies?" Kate suddenly exclaimed, surprising everyone. Clumsily, she pushed her empty plate away, then did the same with Spencer's half-full one. "We're done eating." Spencer opened his mouth to protest, but the cub kicked him under the table.

"Please?" he asked the Weavers, sounding as cheerful as possible as he massaged his shin. *This had better be good.*

27

"Would you hurry up, already?" Kate whispered urgently from the door of Spencer's bedroom. Spencer pulled on a sweatshirt. Bunny had insisted that he put on warmer clothing if he was going to see the fireflies, but he had a feeling that Kate's abrupt request to leave dinner didn't have anything to do with fireflies at all.

"All right, let's go," he said, rejoining Kate. The cub took off down the hallway and up the stairs. As soon as they hit the path outside the Weavers' house, she started to explain. "I remembered at dinner," she said as they rushed down the path toward the center of Bearhaven. "Aldo *always* had Friday night sessions when he was training for the Bear Guard! Reggie and I followed him once to see what it was like, so I know exactly where we can hide."

Instead of following the path through Bearhaven's center and down to the river's edge, Kate turned right at Raymond's Café and led Spencer out toward an open field. Lanterns were just being lit around the field, illuminating the open space. Kate suddenly picked up speed. "Hurry! They're about to start!"

Spencer raced to keep up with Kate, following as she darted into the woods on one side of the field. Crouching together behind a tree, Spencer poked his head around one side and Kate poked hers around the other. A group of at least twenty bears jogged onto the field.

"Whatever they do, you do, got it?" Kate whispered.

"Okay," Spencer whispered back. His pulse was racing with excitement. "But what are they going to do?"

"I have no idea . . ." Kate didn't take her eyes off the Bear Guard recruits. The bears fanned out along one end of the field, then each of the recruits turned and disappeared behind a boulder. "Uh-oh . . ."

"What?" Spencer hissed. He'd thought those boulders were just the far wall of the field . . . Why were they suddenly moving? And where had the recruits gone?

"Boulder rolling," Kate answered. Her voice sounded grave. *Oh.*

Silently, Spencer and Kate watched the boulders roll toward them. Some of the boulders rolled more quickly than others, and some recruits seemed to struggle to get their boulders moving at all at first, but inch by inch, the recruits and their boulders approached. When they were close enough that Spencer could hear the bears straining behind the enormous round rocks, his heart sank. *I have to do . . . that?* A muzzle bumped his shoulder. Kate motioned for him to follow her deeper into the trees.

"Okay," she said slowly, once they were far enough from the field not to risk being overheard. "First, we need a boulder—"

"Kate!" How did she expect him to roll a boulder when *bears* had trouble doing it?

"You can do this, Spencer Plain!" Kate yelled. Then she clapped a paw over her BEAR-COM. "Let's find a boulder," she continued more quietly, scanning the darkening wooded area around them. *Maybe she's right,* Spencer thought. *Maybe I can do this.* He didn't have to be a bear to be good at Bear Stealth, so why did he have to be a bear to be good at this? He didn't have a bear's strength, but he'd find his own way . . .

"Aha! That one looks perfect!"

Spencer followed Kate's gaze. Between two trees sat a round boulder, smaller than the ones he'd seen the recruits using, but bigger than he'd hoped, and he wouldn't call it perfect.

"Maybe it's too late for boulder rolling after all," he said, faking a yawn. "It's getting pretty dark anyway." How could he roll the boulder anywhere if he wouldn't be able to see it in another five minutes?

"Wait here." Kate scooted back the way they came, leaving Spencer alone with the boulder. He walked over to it. The top of the boulder was above his knees, and he knew it was going to be heavy.

"Might as well try while no one's looking," he muttered. Spencer pushed against the boulder with all his strength. His sneakers slid through the dirt and his legs threatened to fly out from underneath him, but he kept pushing. The boulder didn't budge. Suddenly, the trees around him were illuminated in a bobbing yellow light. Spencer spun around.

Kate had the handle of a lantern in her mouth, the light shining brightly. Lifting onto her hind legs, she stood as tall as she could to hang the lantern on a nearby tree limb.

"Where'd you get that?"

She grinned and dropped back to all fours. "I borrowed it! Some guards they'll make—I swiped it right out from under their boulder-rolling noses!"

Spencer sighed. Now that they had plenty of light, there were no excuses left. He turned back to the boulder. Pushing hadn't gotten him anywhere. There had to be some other way . . . A way that didn't depend on his muscles alone.

Spencer circled the boulder. What would Dad do? Or Uncle Mark? Together they could have this boulder rolling in minutes, Spencer was sure of it. He loved watching Dad and Uncle Mark work together. Especially when they were working in the garage on the car that would one day be Spencer's. A year ago, when Spencer's grandfather died, he'd left a 1965 Mustang behind. It didn't run, but Dad and Uncle Mark had it towed to the Plains' garage. They'd taken the whole thing apart—just like Spencer had done with his computer project—and piece by piece they were putting it back together. They were going to make it drive again, and when Spencer turned eighteen, it would be his . . . as long as he didn't spill the beans to Mom, who didn't like fast cars and thought the Mustang was for Uncle Mark.

Whenever he could, Spencer sat in the garage with Dad and Uncle Mark while they worked on the car, studying everything they did. Spencer searched his memory for any piece of information he'd learned in the garage that might help him now.

Kate interrupted Spencer's thoughts. "Well? Are you going to try?"

"Yes, I'm going to try," Spencer muttered, wishing that the boulder was perched on the edge of a steep hill. Then, he got an idea. Scanning the ground, Spencer grabbed a flat rock. Kneeling in front of the boulder, he used the rock as a shovel, digging into the ground to create a small hill. Rolling the boulder downhill would be a whole lot easier than rolling it across flat ground.

"Spencer, I don't think—" Kate started.

"I just have to move it, right?" Spencer dug deeper.

"Well, I guess so." Kate stepped closer to watch. After a few more minutes, Spencer sat back on his heels. Now the ground in front of the boulder sloped downward into a hole. He didn't have the strength to roll the boulder far, but if he just got it moving a little, it would roll as far down as the slope he'd dug. Spencer got up and ran to the other side of the boulder. Throwing all of his weight against the rock, he pushed it toward the slope. Nothing happened.

He needed a tool, something to help him get leverage to push the boulder. Something like a crowbar . . . Spencer thought back to the garage again. "Really, it's just a lever," Dad had said, before drawing a diagram of how a lever worked.

Spencer saw a thick broken tree branch lying in a pile of leaves and dragged it to the boulder. He scooped out another shallow hole under this side of the boulder with his digging rock and then managed to jam one end of the branch into the hole. He grabbed a larger rock and positioned it next to the boulder, sandwiching the branch and holding it in place. The whole thing looked like a seesaw, with the boulder weighing down one end of the branch and the other end sticking up into the air. *Please work.*

Spencer knew if he could push down on the end of the branch that stuck up into the air, it would cause the end of the branch that was sandwiched under the boulder to lift up, causing the boulder to tip over the edge of the slope he'd dug. *It'll roll downward from there!*

"So, are you . . ." Kate started.

"Just wait." The branch stuck up into the air in front of him, the lever he needed to push down. Its highest point was right at his chest. He grabbed onto it with both hands.

Spencer pushed down on the lever. He could feel it straining under the weight of the boulder, and pushed harder. Out of the corner of his eye, he saw the boulder start to move. He threw all of his weight into pushing the lever. "Come on!" he yelled through gritted teeth.

Crash! The branch smashed to the ground and Spencer fell on top of it.

"You did it!" Kate cried. Spencer sat up. The boulder had moved! It was sitting a foot away, at the bottom of the slope he'd dug. The lever had worked. He'd done it.

28

"Push it, Plain!" Fred Crossburger shouted. Spencer stood waist deep in the river, swinging one arm over his head and lifting his opposite knee out of the water in what Fred called a "vine climber." He switched sides and shot an annoyed look at Kate, who pretended not to notice as she followed along with the other bears in the water.

Kate had rushed him out of the Weavers' house at the crack of dawn, assuring him that there was an early Saturday morning Bear Guard workout that they couldn't miss. Rubbing the sleep from his eyes, he'd followed the cub down to the riverside, but rather than the Bear Guard's sunrise swim, they'd found Fred Crossburger preparing for his first water aerobics class of the day.

"I thought they met right here . . ." Kate had said, swinging her head from side to side. There were no recruits to be found, just half a dozen groggy bears wading into the river.

"Look at this," Fred Crossburger had cried as he strode out onto the dock. "Some brave rookies, ready for a workout! You'll have to show them how it's done!" He'd motioned Spencer and Kate toward the water as his class cheered, encouraging them not to worry about the chilly temperature.

Kate tried to explain her mistake to the trainer, but it was no use. Into the water they'd gone.

Now, Spencer felt ridiculous as he shimmied around in the river in his jeans, "scooping salmon" and "reaching for treetops" as best as he could.

"The recruits are probably doing the same stuff, anyway," Kate whispered to Spencer. "It's conditioning!"

Just then, a group of bears came into sight. Walking along the riverbank, a few had towels slung around their necks and some paused to shake water out of their fur. *The recruits from last night!* Spencer jabbed Kate with his elbow. They watched the recruits pass, then disappear through a break in the trees.

"Come on!" Spencer dashed out of the water with Kate close behind. He grabbed his shirt and shoes and socks from the riverbank, and tugged them onto his soaking wet body as quickly as he could. Ignoring Fred's loud demands that they never give up on their fitness goals and get back in the water, Spencer and Kate slipped through the trees.

After a few minutes of searching, Spencer saw the bears up ahead. He ducked behind the closest tree and watched Kate do the same nearby. The recruits stood in a group in the middle of a small clearing, waiting for something. All of a sudden, a whistle blew. Spencer leaned out from behind his tree to get a glimpse of the next training exercise.

It was worse than boulder rolling. Way worse.

Kate crept over to Spencer. "You do what they do, remember?"

Spencer gulped. He remembered, but he *really* wished they were doing anything other than climbing.

Kate looked up at the tree they were hiding behind. "How about this one?" Spencer followed her gaze. The smooth black-and-white bark of the birch looked slippery and uninviting. He touched his jade bear.

It wasn't that he was afraid of climbing. What he minded was being too far off the ground, and what he was afraid of was falling. Spencer didn't know why, but whenever he climbed—like on the rope in gym class—he got a horrible feeling. A weird memory he couldn't place would fill his head, and he'd see images of things he knew had happened but that he couldn't fully remember.

"Spencer?" Kate peered out from behind the tree again. "Okay, here's what they're doing," she said, then hopped onto the tree and climbed up into the branches. She moved from branch to branch until she'd gone as high as she could. After a moment, she climbed back down. "They're being timed, so they're doing it faster, but I think you should just climb as high as you can, okay?"

Spencer didn't say anything. He considered using the extra weight of his wet jeans as an excuse not to climb the tree, or the fact that his shoes might be slick from the river water dripping down his legs.

"Well, what are you waiting for?" Kate interrupted his thoughts.

He gave the jade bear an extra squeeze. *I'm waiting for a harness, or a trampoline, or a net to catch me.*

But before he could come up with an excuse not to climb the tree, Spencer hoisted himself onto the trunk. Wrapping his legs around it, he scooted upward, a few inches at a time. He tried to use his feet to lever himself higher, but the soles of his sneakers slipped against the flat bark, and he lost his grip, bumping roughly back down to the ground.

"Take your shoes off," Kate suggested quietly. "You'll be able to grip the tree better."

She was just trying to be helpful, but Spencer couldn't help feeling annoyed. He kicked off his sneakers and pulled off his now-soggy socks, then gripped the tree again with his arms and legs. Slowly, he started to climb. Kate was right: It was way easier with bare feet.

Climbing higher and higher, Spencer hoped that weird feeling wouldn't happen again, whatever it was . . . As long as he didn't think about falling, maybe—but then it hit him— that nauseating, scattered, mystery memory. "No. Go away," Spencer groaned, but it didn't help. Clinging to the tree with every ounce of his strength, the images flashed through his head—blood, a glint of metal, and the black earth racing up to meet him as he plunged through leaves and branches.

Spencer was halfway up the tree trunk, frozen in place. The memory only took an instant to come and go, but it left him with an awful, dizzying feeling of panic.

"All the way up! Just like a bear!" Kate whispered up to him.

"Kate," he croaked, embarrassed by his lingering fear. "I'm coming back down now." Willing himself to move again, Spencer carefully made his way to the ground where Kate waited. The cub looked him over with concern as he put his damp socks and shoes back on.

"Did you scratch your feet?" she asked. "Mom told me that you have to wear shoes because your feet are too soft. I shouldn't have told you to take them off." She sat back on her haunches and waited for him to answer, a worried look on her face.

"No, it's not my feet. It's not your fault." Spencer looked down at his sneakers and fiddled with the laces. "My arms just got tired. All that boulder rolling last night." He forced a hushed laugh.

Kate brightened. "Or all of those trout trappers!" She swept alternating claws toward the ground rapidly, miming one of Fred's favorite moves. Kate stopped swinging her arms and checked that they hadn't been heard by the Bear Guard recruits. Nobody seemed to have noticed them. "You did *great,*" she said to Spencer emphatically. "Come on, we should get home before Jo-Jo and Winston eat all of our breakfast."

Spencer looked up at the cheerful cub. He wished Kate could come on the bear rescue, too. They made a good team, and Spencer would feel better having her around.

He shook the thought from his head. He needed to focus on his parents. He needed to be brave on his own. He jumped to his feet. "Last one there's a rotten carcass!"

29

Jo-Jo and Winston were still asleep when Spencer and Kate walked into the Weavers' house. Bunny had laid out several bowls of berries in the kitchen, and on the table, where it couldn't be missed, sat a shiny human-sized spoon.

"We've done Bear Stealth, boulder rolling, and climbing," Spencer said as he scooped a spoonful of berries and honey out of the basin in front of him.

"Don't forget the extra conditioning that Fred Crossburger gave us!"

"Right. *That* was helpful." Spencer rolled his eyes. "What's next?"

"Technology and Rescue Ragayo!"

Without his computer project, Spencer wasn't sure how he could practice his technology skills. He didn't think anyone would lend him their BEAR-COM to tinker with, and getting back into the Lab to poke around with the equipment seemed too risky . . . All that left was . . .

"*Salmon King!*" Kate gasped.

Can BEAR-COMs read minds?

"It's impossible to erase old scores on *Salmon King*," the cub explained. "Even Jo-Jo's really low scores from when he was way worse than Winston are still saved. You could try to change it somehow . . ."

"That's perfect! If I can hack into the game, it'll *prove* that I could pass technology training!"

"But we have to do it now. Before Jo-Jo and Winston wake up." Kate gulped down the berries in her bowl. Spencer followed her lead, and within minutes, he was bent over one of the *Salmon King* controllers, figuring out how it worked.

By the time Jo-Jo and Winston wrestled each other into the room an hour later and turned on *Salmon King* to play, Spencer had erased the game's score history, proving to himself and to Kate that they didn't need to spend any more time on technology training. The only score history that popped onto the screen said *Kate—Salmon King—1,000,000 Salmon Caught.*

"Kate!" Jo-Jo had shouted. But Kate and Spencer were already racing out the door, satisfied that Spencer had proven his technology skills.

Spencer followed Kate through Bearhaven, wondering where she'd take him to practice Rescue Ragayo. Finally, she plopped down in the middle of the quiet school yard. *Of course!* There probably wasn't anyone at his school back home, either. It was a Saturday after all.

"Okay, so what words do I need to know?" he asked, diving into the training.

Kate tilted her head thoughtfully. "Well, I'm not sure, but if it's called Rescue Ragayo, then words you'd need in a rescue, I guess."

"So, *safe . . . come . . .*" He started brainstorming.

"*Go . . . attack . . . fast . . . now . . .*" Kate added.

"Attack?" I will have to be really careful with that one.

"Well, more like, 'fight back,' but if there are bad guys chasing you—"

"Right, got it." Spencer cut her off. *Let's hope it doesn't come to that.*

Kate scrambled around to sit facing Spencer, her hind legs sprawled out in front of her. "Let's start with *go*. Are you ready?"

"Ready." He sat up straighter. He was about to learn a secret language that Mom and Dad had been speaking for years.

"Go." Kate's BEAR-COM translated. "Oops!" She pushed the red button on her device to turn it off. *"Grauk."*

"Grauk," Spencer imitated.

Kate shook her head and growled the word again.

"Grauk," he tried in a deeper voice. Kate giggled and pushed in the green button on her BEAR-COM.

"No, it's not supposed to come from your snout—I mean your *nose*." She put a paw on his chest, accidentally knocking him backward. "Imagine you're a bear," she continued once Spencer had righted himself. "Think about the sounds bubbling up from your stomach and out through your throat." She switched her BEAR-COM off. They went back and forth again and again, but Spencer still didn't get it right.

"What's the *difference*?!" Spencer finally exclaimed.

"You have to growl more," Kate answered. "Try again, but put your hands like this." She placed one paw against her belly, and the other up to her throat. Spencer did the same. "Remember, more growl." Kate demonstrated again. *"Grauk."*

Spencer heard it differently this time.

He tried to imagine the sounds coming from deep in the pit of his stomach, rumbling up through his throat. *"Grauk."*

Kate nodded vigorously, spouting excited Ragayo until she had her BEAR-COM turned back on. "That's it! You've got it!"

"Grauk," he said again, feeling the word build up and move out of him, hearing the growl.

They continued on to the next word, *shala,* for "safe," and slowly, Spencer got the hang of it. By the time they'd repeated each of the words they'd brainstormed several times, he understood how the words should feel, and he could form the sounds with little effort.

"One last one!" Kate switched off her BEAR-COM before Spencer could ask what this new word would mean. *"Anbranda."*

"Anbranda," he repeated. "What does it mean?"

"'Warrior for your family,'" she said, dropping her paw from her device. "Like someone who'd fight to protect you or the bears you love." Then, scrambling to her feet, she added, "It works for 'friend,' too. Seems like a good one to know."

"Anbranda," Spencer said again.

30

The only way for Spencer to prove that he should be included on the rescue mission was to surprise Uncle Mark and the Weavers with a demonstration of all of the skills he and Kate had practiced in training. As soon as Uncle Mark arrived for breakfast that morning, Kate steered everyone over to the couches where Spencer was waiting, determined to earn his place on the rescue team.

Now Spencer stood in front of the Weavers' fireplace, watching Professor Weaver's, Bunny's, and Uncle Mark's faces as he finished explaining the inner workings of the *Salmon King* game he'd hacked. Kate looked on, nodding emphatically at every word Spencer said.

"Very interesting, Spencer," Professor Weaver said, as though trying to puzzle out *why* the *Salmon King* game had to be hacked at all, or why they were hearing about it now when they were supposed to be having breakfast, then sending Uncle Mark off on the rescue mission.

Kate caught Spencer's look and launched into the next skill.

"Safe!" she prompted.

"*Shala!*" Spencer translated.

"Go!"

Spencer growled, *"Grauk!"*

"Fast!"

"Gal!"

"Attack!"

"Kate!" Bunny exclaimed before Spencer could recite the word in Ragayo. "Why on earth would you teach Spencer to say 'attack'?"

"It's Rescue Ragayo, Mom," Kate said matter-of-factly. Uncle Mark raised an eyebrow. The cub pressed on. "In addition to being trained in Rescue Ragayo, Spencer Plain can do anything a bear can do. For example . . ." She hesitated, anxiously searching for a word. *Come on, Kate,* Spencer willed, eager to get to Bear Stealth. "Yesterday, Fred Crossburger himself called Spencer aerobic!" *Aerobic?*

Uncle Mark chuckled. "Is that so?"

"More importantly," Spencer rushed on, "I can do things bears and adults *can't* do."

"Let's see it!" Kate chimed. "Everybody close your eyes."

"Kate Dora Weaver, what on earth?"

"Spence, I really have to get going." Uncle Mark looked at his watch. "Maybe we could save the rest of this . . . presentation for when I'm back?"

"Five more minutes," Spencer said. "Please close your eyes." Uncle Mark sighed, then closed his eyes. Professor Weaver nodded and did the same. After a small sigh, Bunny let her eyelids fall shut. As soon as she did, Spencer dropped to the floor and slipped underneath the only empty couch in the room. It was a tight squeeze, but he could fit his entire body beneath it, and the upholstery hung down around him, hiding him completely.

"Open your eyes and behold Spencer, master of Bear Stealth!" Kate announced. A moment of silence passed.

"Spence?" Uncle Mark's muffled voice traveled down to Spencer.

"Spencer, why don't you come on out now." It was Professor Weaver.

"No!" Kate protested. "You have to find him."

"Kate," Bunny warned. Even from under the couch, Spencer could tell that Bunny wasn't amused, but she hadn't seen where he'd gone yet. He slipped out from under the couch. "Oh!" she cried upon seeing him. "My goodness, I can't believe you fit under there!" Bunny looked from the couch to Spencer and back again. Professor Weaver seemed impressed, but Uncle Mark just watched calmly as Kate pressed on.

"He climbs just as well as he hides!" On cue, Spencer approached the support beam in one corner of the room. Polished to a smooth column, the beam looked as though it had been carved from a tree trunk and put there as much for decoration as for ceiling support. Spencer grasped it with both hands and hoisted himself up, but just as he started to climb, Professor Weaver's voice stopped him.

"All right, son," the bear said. "Why don't you tell us what this is all about."

Spencer dropped to the floor and looked at the professor. *Not yet!* He wanted to shout. *You have to give me a chance!*

"But we have so much more—" Kate started. Bunny cut her off.

"I think an explanation is in order, dear." She patted the space on the couch next to her. Kate padded over and took a seat beside her mother, then sank back into the cushions to sulk. Spencer stood up, but didn't move to join everyone on the cluster of couches.

He'd done all he possibly could to get ready for this. Yesterday, he and Kate had practiced Bear Stealth again after lunch, and Rescue Ragayo right after that. He'd even given climbing another shot—not that it went any better the second time around—and he'd mastered using his mind and resources to move a boulder when his strength wasn't enough. He'd been so exhausted last night that he hadn't said much at dinner with the Weavers. Then, when he finally crashed into bed, he'd heard paper crinkle beneath him.

After re-reading the letter from Mom telling him why his parents had given him the jade bear, Spencer had decided he wasn't taking no for an answer today. He was going on this mission.

"I want to go with you, Uncle Mark," he said calmly. "I know you think I'm just a kid, but that could be a good thing. I can hide where no one else can. I can move boulders by building a lever just like Dad taught me. I'm really good with technology, and I can speak some Rescue Ragayo now. Those are all things the bears training for the guard need to do, and I can do them." He looked pleadingly at his uncle.

"Spence, I'm sorry," Uncle Mark said, looking Spencer in the eye. "I just don't think it's a good idea . . ."

"The risk is too high, dear," said Bunny.

"I can help save Ro Ro and the cubs. And if I could just see the place, I know I'd be able to—"

"Spencer." Uncle Mark stopped him. "The answer is no."

Why didn't Uncle Mark understand? He turned to Professor Weaver. *Maybe there's still a chance . . .*

But the professor shook his head. "I'm afraid that settles it, son."

"This isn't fair!" Kate shouted. "He *trained*!"

Bunny hushed her cub. The conversation was over. Spencer reached into his pocket and took hold of the jade bear.

Bears trust their instincts, his mother had written in her letter. *They use their senses to understand what's happening around them, then they do what they know is right.*

"Maybe Spencer could at least see you to the station, Mark?" Bunny suggested after a moment, her voice full of sympathy.

Uncle Mark relaxed, the tension in the room lifting. "Yeah, that'd be all right."

"Can Kate come?" Spencer asked quickly. His uncle shrugged.

"I don't see why not."

Spencer shot Kate a look. *This isn't over yet.*

31

Spencer had asked a lot of questions over the past few days, but as they made their way down the dirt path and into the clearing where he'd first met the Weavers, it occurred to him that he'd never asked Uncle Mark how he'd gotten from the abandoned railway tunnel where he'd parked the Porsche all the way into Bearhaven. Without a bear to carry him up the first tree to the hologram-covered bridge, it would have been impossible for Uncle Mark to come in the same way Spencer had. Besides, B.D. had said that they rarely entered Bearhaven by the bridge in the trees.

Spencer watched as B.D. approached the very same tree that had dropped him into the clearing. The bear touched a concealed button on the bark of the tree, and the door slid open, revealing the smooth, hollowed-out space inside the trunk, and the platform that Spencer knew would rise to the knothole above.

He wanted to ask Uncle Mark now, but B.D. was already cranky. "I wasn't aware I'd be chaperoning a field trip today," the bear had huffed when Spencer and Kate followed Uncle Mark out of the Weavers' house.

Spencer caught Kate's eye and pointed up, questioning if they'd go back out the same way he'd entered Bearhaven. The cub shook her head and pointed down. Apparently the clearing wasn't the only stop the tree elevator made.

"It's a train," Kate whispered, but not as quietly as Spencer would have liked. Uncle Mark turned. He was wearing his leather jacket and had an army-green canvas bag slung over one shoulder. He didn't look anything like a spy—or an *operative,* as everyone kept calling it—just his usual, cool self.

"Everything okay?" he asked Spencer. "You've been pretty quiet."

"Yeah," Spencer answered. "Just didn't know you were going by train, that's all." Uncle Mark didn't say anything for a moment, and Spencer thought he saw some regret, or maybe sympathy, in his uncle's eyes.

B.D. grumbled, standing impatiently beside the open door. "Did you expect us to *walk* to Stantonville?" he asked gruffly. In an only slightly kinder voice he added, "Even a train can't take us anywhere unless we get on it. Shall we go down?" B.D. waved them all into the hollow tree.

Kate, who so far had been following Spencer's lead, staying quiet and well-behaved, bounded forward onto the platform.

"Reggie's going to be so jealous!" she gushed to B.D., who pretended not to hear her. "I don't think *any* of the other Bearhaven cubs have seen the TUBE! Not the ones born here, I mean." She chattered on. Spencer followed, then Uncle Mark and B.D., who took up the last of the space inside the tree trunk. "Spencer!" Kate called as the door slid shut and they were cast into darkness. "Do you know what *TUBE* stands for?"

Before Spencer could answer, the platform started to drop, just like the one in the Lab, faster than any elevator he'd ever been on. He held his breath. It almost felt like falling—

"Traveling. Underground. Bear. Explorers!" Kate chirped into the dark. Uncle Mark laughed, and B.D. gave an exasperated sigh, then the platform lurched to a halt.

"Actually," B.D. said as the door slid open, "it's Transcontinental Underground Bear Expressway."

Spencer stepped off the platform and into a train station buzzing with activity. Three bears stood beside a sleek white train, polishing its tinted windows until they gleamed like new pennies, pinkish-brown and shining. Rolling carts stacked high with boxes sat on the smooth stone platform, waiting to be loaded. Some of the boxes were marked with a red cross. *Medical supplies,* Spencer assumed. Some were marked as containing food or drink, and the rest were marked with various symbols that Spencer couldn't take the time to decipher.

A medium-sized black bear who Spencer didn't recognize stood at the first car of the train, talking animatedly and motioning toward the sloped front window. A silver cuff on her wrist caught the light. *A member of the Bear Guard.* The bear shifted, revealing Aldo, who stood beside her.

"Aldo!" Kate squealed. B.D. quieted her.

"Better let him focus, young lady," he explained. "Aldo's learning to run a TUBE security check."

B.D., Uncle Mark, and the cub had filed out of the elevator behind Spencer. He turned just in time to see the door slide shut. Underground, the entrance to the elevator didn't look anything like the wide tree trunk that they'd entered above

ground; instead it had stainless steel doors with a button beside them. *We're really far below ground,* Spencer thought, and looked up. The ceiling, which at first looked like it was painted a marbled brown, was actually made of glass, allowing the natural webbing of intertwined roots to show through. The roots spread out above them like a canopy.

Uncle Mark slung an arm around Spencer's shoulders. "She's a beauty, isn't she?" He beamed at the train.

"Yeah," Spencer said. He had to figure out how to get *onto* that beauty without anyone else noticing, and then he had to figure out how to *stay* on that beauty long enough for turning back to be out of the question.

And before he could stop himself, he had to ask. "But *how*? Where did it come from?" Had Mom and Dad built

Bearhaven *and* a railroad? Out of the corner of his eye Spencer could see Kate sneaking down the platform toward Aldo. B.D. grumbled and went after her.

"Your parents and I refurbished an old rail line," Uncle Mark explained. "It had been out of use for years. I bought it at auction, posing as an old geezer who collected train stuff as a hobby." He paused and then, in a wavering old man's voice, said, "It was my 'crown jewel.'" Spencer thought his uncle sounded pretty convincing, and he would have loved to see Uncle Mark in disguise. He was so used to seeing his uncle look like he'd just stepped out of a men's fashion magazine that he couldn't imagine him as an old man. "It's got tunnels and arteries all over the country and up into Canada," Uncle Mark continued. "We closed or hid all of the aboveground entrances, basically taking it entirely off the map. The hidden tunnel I mentioned the other night? That's one of the old stations. I parked the Porsche there and rode the TUBE the rest of the way into Bearhaven."

"Wow." Spencer couldn't help but be impressed. "Can I see the inside?"

Uncle Mark glanced down at his watch. "We can do a quick tour, but you have to stick with me. Exploring on your own will have to wait for another time, got it?"

Spencer's excitement threatened to give him away. "Got it," he said, sounding as serious as he could.

"Good. Then let's start in the front. You're never going to believe what your mom did with the interior."

32

Careful to look as glum as possible, Spencer thanked Uncle Mark for the quick tour and stepped out of the train. He set off down the platform to find Kate. Having memorized the order of the train's cars as Uncle Mark showed him around, Spencer had a plan, but they had to move fast. B.D. and Uncle Mark were heading up to the engine car to confirm the route, the last of the boxes had been loaded into the cargo car, and the crew of bears who had been preparing the train for departure had disappeared through a door on one side of the platform that read *Maintenance Staff Only*.

He looked around quickly and spotted Kate sitting on a wide stone bench swinging her legs, listening to Aldo recite the guidelines for a TUBE security check to his supervisor.

"Come on," Spencer whispered urgently when he was close enough. Kate hopped off the bench and followed him back toward the train. Spencer headed straight for the cargo car. The last car in the row, the cargo car's door was open and locked into place above the car, like a beetle's open wing ready to fly.

On the walk from the Weavers' house to the TUBE, Spencer had been able to tell Kate that he was going on the mission, he just wasn't sure how yet. She'd shaken her head, trying to dissuade him, but they'd been too close behind B.D. and Uncle Mark, and Spencer had gestured for her to be quiet.

"I need your help," Spencer whispered now as they approached the cargo car. "I'm going to hide on the train."

"Are you *crazy?*" she asked quietly. "What if they're right? What if it is too dangerous?" she rushed on. "Aren't you scared to leave Bearhaven?"

"I'm not scared." Spencer stopped walking. He looked up and down the platform, but only Aldo and his supervisor were in view, and both bears had their backs turned. *This is it,* he thought. If they got caught now, he wouldn't have another chance.

He gave his jade bear a quick squeeze. *Bears are devoted animals, Spencer,* Mom had written in the letter, *and so are the Plains. No matter how far or how often we travel, your father and I will always come home to you.* Spencer pulled his hand from his pocket. This time, he was going to have to bring them home.

As soon as the thought came, he shook it away. This mission wasn't really meant to save Mom and Dad, but it was a start. For now, he'd have to help his parents by finishing the bear rescue they'd begun.

Spencer checked once more that nobody was watching, then looked at Kate, jerked his head toward the cargo car's open door, and jumped through it. The cub hurtled in after him, landing so hard that the car shook underneath them. He glared at her.

"Sorry," she whispered, but was too captivated by the inside of the train to seem very apologetic. *This isn't even one of the cool cars,* Spencer thought as Kate sniffed at the boxes piled high around them.

He went to one of the stacks and started moving things. "What are you doing?" Kate asked. Spencer took a medium-sized box off a larger one and put it on the floor, then opened the large box and started pulling out the blankets he found inside, stuffing them back behind other stacks of boxes.

"I'm going to get in here," he answered once the box was empty and the blankets had all been hidden. "Once I'm in, close the top, and put that box back on the pile." He pointed to the box he'd put on the floor. "It's not heavy. It won't crush me or anything."

Spencer started to scramble up the side of the box, but it was harder than he'd thought. Kate pushed her head against it, holding the box steady so that Spencer could climb all the way up and slide in. "Thanks," he said once he righted himself. "Oh, I almost forgot. Once you've hidden me, go to the engine—the front car—and find Uncle Mark. Tell him I was so upset that I wasn't allowed to go with them that I didn't think I could even say good-bye. Say I took the elevator up and went back alone."

Kate nodded slowly, like she hadn't decided yet if she would let Spencer go hidden away in the boxes.

"This is what we trained for," Spencer urged the cub. She was the only chance he had. "I'm ready, *anbranda.*"

"Okay," she said at last.

Spencer crouched down while Kate closed the box flaps over him. He heard her replace the other box and then pause. "Good luck, Spencer Plain," she whispered, then stepped away. Spencer listened to the light thumping of her feet as she ran off the train to deliver his message.

Long minutes passed. Spencer waited silently in the dark of the box, desperate to feel the train begin to move. The plan *had* to work! Uncle Mark *had* to believe that Spencer returned to the Weavers' alone!

After what felt like hours, Spencer heard a faint *hushhhh* and then a muted *click*. It took him a moment to place the sound, but when he did, he had to stop himself from letting out a cheer.

The door of the cargo car had slid down and locked into place.

Spencer felt a gentle lurch, and the boxes shifted around him. The train was leaving the station. They were on their way!

33

"Welcome aboard."

Startled, Spencer looked up into the friendly eyes of a bear he didn't recognize. Only seconds ago he'd heard someone enter the cargo car and approach the box he was hiding in. He'd stiffened, his box shifting around him as the one on top of it was removed. Before he could do anything, the flaps of cardboard above him had been pulled apart.

"I'm Marguerite, and my nose never lies." She gave an exaggerated sniff. "Right now it's telling me that *you're* not supposed to be here." With a little blue cap perched on top of her head and a smile on her face, Marguerite looked practically cheerful to have discovered a stowaway on the train. Spencer sighed. Uncle Mark and B.D. wouldn't be nearly so happy to see him, but being discovered *was* part of his plan. He just hoped they were far enough along in the trip that they couldn't turn around and take him back to Bearhaven.

"Hi," he answered, standing up and brushing himself off. "I'm Spencer."

"Is that so?" Marguerite replied, and in one quick movement, she scooped Spencer out of the box with a clawless paw and deposited him on his feet in front of her. She straightened her navy vest and patted a few of the gold-trimmed pockets lightly as though checking that all of the contents were still securely in place. "Pleased to meet you, Spencer." He blinked at her, reeling from having been moved around like a sack of potatoes. "This way!" Marguerite trilled as she left the cargo car. Spencer followed. *Here we go . . .*

They left the cargo car, passed through the medical car, and entered the wardrobe car—at least, that's what Uncle Mark had called it on his whirlwind tour of the train. Full-length mirrors and makeup tables lined either side of the car, and on each end there were closets. Uncle Mark hadn't told him what was in the closets, and Spencer couldn't imagine why the TUBE needed a wardrobe car at all, but he didn't ask Marguerite. He was too busy coming up with ways to make a case for himself.

Marguerite and Spencer entered the passenger car together, but Spencer stayed tucked behind the bear, trying to delay the moment when Uncle Mark and B.D. realized what he'd done.

"There you are, Marguerite. We thought we'd lost you." The voice was B.D.'s, but the tone was one that Spencer had never heard the authoritative bear use before. He sounded . . . playful. But then Marguerite stepped aside, revealing Spencer, and any possibility of playfulness was sucked right out of the train.

For a moment, everyone was silent.

Avoiding B.D.'s eyes, Spencer looked around. On the tour with Uncle Mark, he'd been impressed by how cool the passenger car's interior was. The seats were pearl-colored and looked like huge nautilus shells. Each chair was topped with a segmented hood and outfitted with a ton of high-tech features. Mom had done an awesome job, but now, under B.D.'s furious gaze, Spencer wished he were anywhere else.

Uncle Mark's legs were poking out of one of the cocoon-like seats. He didn't have a view of Spencer from where he sat, but something about the deathly silence that had fallen over the car got his attention. He leaned around the side of his seat, his neck craning to follow B.D.'s glare.

"Spencer!"

"As you can see, gentlemen," Marguerite said quickly, "I've made a new friend. Now, I think I'll leave you three alone to sort this out. But don't you worry, I'll be back in, say . . ." She looked at a huge gold watch on her wrist. "Half an hour? Refreshments and snacks then, all right? All right!" With that, she turned and sashayed out of the car.

"I'm . . . I'm sorry." Spencer broke the silence.

"Are you?" B.D. snarled.

"Spencer, this is really crossing a line." Uncle Mark's tone was hard. "I thought I'd made myself clear."

"You did . . ." Spencer began. "But . . . I guess . . . Well . . . I don't think I made *myself* clear." His voice shook a little. B.D. gave a low, warning growl.

Follow your instincts.

Spencer pulled the jade bear from his pocket and held it out for B.D. and Uncle Mark to see. "This is the bear Mom and Dad gave me when I turned eight. It's always with me, because they aren't. When I'm nervous or scared, I hold on to it and remember that I can be like a bear." He looked B.D. in the eye. "That I can be brave and strong and smart. But this bear is more than that." He looked at his uncle. "I've been learning about bears my whole life. In our family, bears are at the center of everything. I mean, Mom and Dad call me their *cub*. Bears are just . . . They're in my blood." He took a deep breath. "The Plains rescue bears, and I'm as much a Plain as Mom and Dad. I'm *coming* on this mission. For my family. To help bring them home." He clutched the jade bear and put it back in his pocket. Then he looked from Uncle Mark to B.D., waiting for the verdict.

B.D.'s demeanor softened ever so slightly. He nodded, then looked to Uncle Mark. Uncle Mark ran a hand through his hair.

"I understand, Spence," he said quietly. "Your determination . . . It's really . . . your parents would be proud."

"Please. I can help. I've even trained to be here."

"If you get hurt, your mom will never forgive me." Uncle Mark shook his head slowly.

"Just wait until you and Dad give me Grandpa's Mustang . . . Might as well get a head start on things she'll never forgive you for, right?"

Uncle Mark laughed. "All right, Spence, you're in."

"All right," B.D. said. "But there's one more thing. I've had just about enough of you showing up in places you're not supposed to be. You need to be where we tell you to be from now on."

Spencer flopped into the seat next to the bear. He was going on the mission. B.D. could have the last word.

34

Spencer woke up inside the pod that his seat had transformed into. Marguerite had showed him how to pull the segmented hood down all the way, then press a button, causing the seat to unfold into a cozy, covered bed. He hadn't meant to fall asleep—he'd just wanted to test out the bed—but now he had no idea how long he'd been sleeping or what time it was.

Pressing the button that had made the seat unfold, Spencer felt his bed rise, tilt forward, and return to its original shape. Pushing the hood up, he opened his pod to the passenger car around him.

Earlier, when they'd all eaten Raymond's boxed dinners, the train car had been bright and inviting. Now, the lights were dimmed.

The hood of Uncle Mark's seat was closed and Spencer could hear soft snoring coming from within. Spencer turned to B.D.'s seat, expecting to see the hood drawn and hear the muted thunder of bear snores. Instead, he found the neighboring chair upright and B.D. awake, sipping from a mug cradled between his front paws.

Something about the way the bear's eyes never left the train's window, even as he sipped his drink, made Spencer think that he shouldn't interrupt B.D.'s thoughts, but instead of pressing the button to turn his chair back into a bed, Spencer accidently pressed one that made music blare out of his headrest. Startled, B.D. turned as Spencer fumbled to shut the music off.

"Sorry," he whispered, once he'd quieted his headrest. "I didn't mean to interrupt . . ."

"There wasn't much to interrupt," B.D. answered, his voice free of its usual gruffness. The bear lifted his mug to his lips, and Spencer noticed that the familiar flash of silver was missing.

"Where are your Bear Guard cuffs?" he asked.

"I don't wear them outside of Bearhaven. If I have to slip into the woods, they can hinder Bear Stealth, or if I have to blend in with other bears—whatever the case may be, it's best if I'm not wearing the cuffs. Marguerite has already put them away for me. She's an important part of the rescue team, you know," he added.

"Well, she's definitely good at sniffing out stowaways."

B.D. chuckled. "Yes, Spencer, she is good at that . . . Of course, not all of the rescue missions use the TUBE, and not all of the rescued bears make Bearhaven their home, but for many, Marguerite is an important part of their journey." B.D. turned back to the window. "A lot of bears have entered Bearhaven on this train over the years, and each of them was greeted with Marguerite's kindness."

"Have you and my parents rescued every single bear who lives in Bearhaven?"

"Besides the bears who've been born in Bearhaven, yes," said B.D., turning back to Spencer. And then, "No, that's not right. There *is* one bear who came to Bearhaven on his own—who wasn't actually rescued, but who escaped from a terrible situation and managed to find us himself. No other bear's done that. Very unusual and very brave. But then, Yude is an unusual and brave bear."

"*Yude?!*" Spencer cried in disbelief, then clapped a hand over his mouth.

B.D. eyed him questioningly.

"He's so . . . *mean*," Spencer said quietly, trying to explain himself. "He doesn't want anything to do with me."

"Yude isn't mean exactly, Spencer. He's gruff. He's impatient. And he's had some painful encounters with humans that have left him suspicious and bitter. But he's also a brilliant strategist—he has to be to have found his own way to Bearhaven. And he wants what's best for the bears there."

"I don't know . . ." Spencer shuddered as he recalled Yude's anger in the council room.

"It's sad, actually, that Yude's never been able to fully understand how good and kind Mark and your parents are." The bear paused for such a long moment that Spencer thought the conversation might be over.

"You know, Spencer, I consider them my family, too—your mom and dad and your uncle." B.D.'s gaze returned to the window. "They saved my life," he said a moment later, as much to the tunnel beyond the window as to Spencer.

"What? When?" Spencer asked carefully. He didn't want to break whatever spell B.D. seemed to be under.

"Before Bearhaven."

Before Bearhaven? *How was that possible, unless—*

"Were you—?"

"One of the first," B.D. said quickly. "One of the mascots."

"From Gutler University?"

B.D. nodded. "I was sold to Gutler with my brother and sister when we were young. They wanted us for mascots, to parade us around at sporting events, but they treated us terribly. The handler—Margo Lalicki, whom your uncle's told you about?" Spencer nodded. "That woman drugged us and kept our teeth and claws filed down to nubs so we had no natural defenses. It made eating painful, not that there was much to eat. They kept us in a cage half the size of this train car, and let us starve." B.D. shook his massive head, as if he was trying to shake the memory away. "Dora was my older sister," he went on. "She protected my brother, John Shirley, and me whenever she could. Even when her own ribs showed, she'd share her food with us. She was smarter than my brother and me, too, and tough." B.D. turned back to Spencer. "Dora would've done well at Bearhaven."

"What happened to her?" Spencer asked, remembering what Uncle Mark had said about the female bear being recaptured at Gutler.

"Dora never made it out." B.D. paused. "Your parents and Mark staged a rescue . . ." He hesitated again before continuing, and when he did, Spencer could tell that the bear was choosing his words carefully. "It was the first rescue, for all of us. Things were bound to go wrong. Dora was the last to be brought to the truck, but before she made it, guard dogs and floodlights surrounded us. We had to leave her. It was the only way any of us would have gotten out." B.D.'s voice was filled with regret. "We knew Dora would've been hurt and angry that things didn't go as we'd planned . . . that she was left behind . . . So at the first opportunity, your mom and dad went back for her. They searched, but couldn't find her. It was like she'd disappeared. All they found was a scrap of her Gutler football jersey."

"Her what?"

"Gutler made us wear green-and-gold jerseys during their football games. We fly the scrap we found from her shirt on the flagpole in Bearhaven, to always remember what we've sacrificed, and what we've gained. And to remember Dora."

Spencer looked down at his hands. He remembered that flag from his tour of Bearhaven, but he never imagined it could mean so much. "And what about your brother?"

"John Shirley? He's out there."

Spencer counted twelve tunnel lights flash past the window before B.D. spoke again. "Bearhaven was never going to be home for John Shirley. After what we'd been through, he wasn't interested in communicating much with humans. He appreciated the rescue and what your family did for him, but he didn't want a lifestyle that too closely resembled theirs. Many bears feel that way."

Spencer nodded, but didn't really know what B.D. meant. Seeming to sense this, B.D. added, "For many of us, Bearhaven is a safe community, but for some, it's a reminder of what we've suffered."

"Do you ever see him? John Shirley?"

"Every now and then," said B.D. "Not often, and I never know which time will be the last. We know how to find each other, though, in case we need to . . . In case either of us finds Dora."

Spencer leaned back in his chair as they lapsed into silence. B.D. understood what it meant to miss your family, to want to save them from something.

Poor Dora, Spencer thought. *After all she'd done to protect her brothers at Gutler, she'd never seen them again.* He wondered where she was, if she was even still alive. He turned to B.D. but found the bear asleep, his empty mug resting between his paws.

35

"A bear in pain is a very dangerous animal," Uncle Mark said, consulting the long list of things that he needed to brief Spencer on before their arrival in Stantonville. Spencer nodded. All morning he'd been careful to keep an expression of total focus on his face, but inside, his mind was racing. His first rescue mission!

The mission would be dangerous, and a huge test, but Spencer still couldn't help thinking how cool it all was. A week ago, he'd been worried about homework and whether or not Evarita would let him order pizza again for dinner. Now, he was a Bearhaven *operative*.

"Ro Ro and her cubs may have had their claws and teeth removed, which means they could be in a great deal of pain," Uncle Mark went on. "And that's just the normal level of risk on a rescue, Spence. We might be up against something bigger with this one. We don't know yet how the bears are affected by the implanted microchips."

Spencer sat across from Uncle Mark at a table in the first car. On the tour, Uncle Mark had shown Spencer that the first car of the train was split in half. The front half housed the engine room and control panel for the TUBE, and the back half was outfitted as a small dining room.

Marguerite had just served Spencer and Uncle Mark each a heaping bowl of oatmeal, brown sugar, and berries. Spencer was happy to see something so human and so delicious, but also surprised. Since arriving in Bearhaven, he'd eaten well, but everything had been made from ingredients that the bears could gather themselves, like fish, honey, and plants from the forest. The food had never involved anything like oatmeal or brown sugar.

Uncle Mark winked at Spencer as he dug in. Oatmeal was Uncle Mark's favorite breakfast.

"Do you bring your own *oatmeal*?" Spencer asked incredulously.

Uncle Mark smiled and made a show of taking a huge, satisfying bite. "Never underestimate the comforts of home, kid."

Marguerite glided over to check on them. "Do you like it, honey?" she asked Spencer. He nodded and gulped down a mouthful of oatmeal. "Good. There's plenty more where that came from. Mark's got quite the supply socked away on this train."

Spencer watched Marguerite make her way down the car to check on B.D., who was sitting alone at another table.

If he didn't know the bear any better, Spencer would have thought B.D. might have a crush on Marguerite. The large bear had been watching her all morning as she moved around the car, acting almost goofy every time she approached. Spencer looked away; maybe a girlfriend was just the thing to make B.D. a little happier and a little less grumpy . . . "—is already there, doing a preliminary sweep of the grounds," Uncle Mark was saying. "So at least we'll have more information going in."

"Wait, what?" Spencer had missed something important.

"The other operative is already there." *There was another operative?* It wouldn't be just him and Uncle Mark going in to get the bears? He pushed away his disappointment. He had to admit it made sense for them to have the extra backup, since B.D. wouldn't actually be in the field with them, unless his physical strength became necessary.

"Who is it?"

A sly smile crossed Uncle Mark's face. "I'm going to let you find out for yourself. Now, back to business. We should be on-site by three o'clock, and the bear baying starts at five. First step is locating Ro Ro and her cubs as quickly as possible. We're not anticipating that the cubs will be involved in the bear baying, but we know that there's also a petting zoo on the premises. It's likely that the cubs will be there. It's your job to confirm that." *Of course,* Spencer thought, *I'm on cub duty.*

"Ro Ro's in the most danger, and we'll have a limited amount of time before they take her in for the five o'clock show, so we'll need to get her out before five. Once Ro Ro is safely in the rescue vehicle, B.D. will be with her to calm her down and explain what's going on, then our other operative is going to make a scene. She'll pretend to discover that the bear is missing and rile up the crowd, convincing them a dangerous bear is on the loose." *She? The other operative was a girl?* "In the midst of the commotion, we'll get the cubs to the rescue vehicle."

"We're just going to walk them to the vehicle? Because everyone will be freaking out?" This might be Spencer's first mission, but even so, that didn't exactly sound like a foolproof plan.

"I know it sounds too simple, but sometimes a simple plan works better than a complicated one. The operative on the ground now is getting a handle on Grady's Grandstand— the operation, the layout—she'll know more, and she'll have what we need when she picks us up." Uncle Mark looked at his watch, then called to Marguerite. "Are we running on time?"

Marguerite stood up quickly from B.D.'s table and straightened her vest. *If bears could blush* . . . Spencer thought, looking from Marguerite to B.D., who was suddenly captivated by the inside of his bowl.

"Yes, absolutely. On time," Marguerite gushed. "Two fifteen p.m. arrival as planned. Anything else?" But before anyone could answer, she scooted over to the farthest table in the room, as though the flowers there needed to be rearranged immediately.

Uncle Mark looked at Spencer and rolled his eyes. Spencer only barely stopped himself from bursting out laughing. "All right, then. We'll get back to the briefing, but for now, we are *much* too good-looking for a rescue mission."

36

The wardrobe car turned out to be just as cool as the rest of the TUBE. One of the closets was for women and the other was for men, but both were huge, as big as five of Spencer's closets at home, and stuffed full of the craziest mix of clothes Spencer had ever seen. There were trunks full of hats, wigs, even fake facial hair. There were racks upon racks of shoes, all worn in just enough to not seem too new.

Spencer pulled open a drawer and quickly slammed it shut. It was filled with rows of . . . noses? He opened the drawer again, slowly. Yes, noses. They looked so real. Pulling open the next drawer, he found ears, and in the one below it, chins. Uncle Mark laughed when Spencer poked an ear, then picked it up, wrinkling his nose, and turned it over in his hand.

"They're prosthetics," Uncle Mark explained. "Like they use on actors."

Spencer returned to the nose drawer and picked one out, fitting it over his own nose. It was rubbery against his skin and way too big, but when he looked in the mirror, it looked natural enough to be creepy. "Can I wear one?"

Uncle Mark laughed. "Not this time. Takes too long to put on properly. We only go that far on advanced missions. This mission should be pretty straightforward."

Spencer returned the nose and browsed through the clothes that hung, tightly packed, from wall to wall. It was like hundreds of strangers had each sent in a complete outfit from their own wardrobes. *Why does Uncle Mark always wear jeans and a leather jacket when he could wear any of this?* Spencer wondered, reaching for a black-and-white-checked velvet jacket.

"Do the bears have a wardrobe closet?"

"No." Uncle Mark started pulling things out for his disguise. "If we need to hide the bears, it usually takes more than a few pieces of extra-large clothing. That's what the special vehicles are for."

To Spencer's disappointment, the new outfit that Uncle Mark had put together looked like the most boring thing his uncle could have picked. "Out you go," Uncle Mark said. "Time for my transformation." Reluctantly, Spencer left the closet.

When Uncle Mark emerged, he looked like someone else completely. Not only had his uncle disguised his real identity, adding a weirdly natural-looking goatee and a dirty white baseball cap with a dried sweat ring around the band, but he looked totally *unremarkable*. Spencer wished his uncle had come up with something a little more exciting, like the police officer's uniform that Spencer had seen, or a suit that would make him look like James Bond, but he understood why Uncle Mark had chosen the outfit he did. Dressed in slightly baggy, worn blue jeans and a tucked-in gray T-shirt with a white logo for Rusty's Crab Shack, Uncle Mark would completely fade into the background. Spencer laughed. "Where's your pickup truck?"

"Very funny." Uncle Mark tossed a bundle of clothes to Spencer. "Let's see how good you look undercover."

Spencer quickly laid everything out in front of him on one of the makeup tables, excited to see what his own disguise would look like. There was a plain white T-shirt, a lightweight plaid flannel shirt, and a navy blue baseball cap with yellow writing: *Sonny's Express*.

"Wow, cool," Spencer said sarcastically.

"Not a lot in your size in here, Spence. I didn't know you'd be joining us, remember?" Uncle Mark winked, then started toward the door. "Change up. We'll be pulling into the station in fifteen minutes. Oh, and mess your hair up a little under the cap."

By the time the TUBE pulled into the station, Spencer had adjusted the flannel shirt about a million times, buttoning it and tucking it into his jeans, then untucking it, then rolling up the sleeves, then down, then unbuttoning it, and on and on. Finally, Uncle Mark walked over.

"You nervous, Spence?" He put his hands on Spencer's shoulders. "You don't have to come if you've changed your mind."

Spencer *was* nervous, more nervous than he'd thought he'd be, but he definitely wasn't going to say so. "Just not sure how this shirt's supposed to look," he mumbled.

"Oh, is that all?" Uncle Mark said, stepping back and looking him over. Spencer knew he wasn't fooling anyone, but he appreciated that his uncle let it go. "Unbuttoned, untucked, sleeves rolled up."

As Spencer adjusted his shirt for the last time, there was a quiet *pop,* followed by a *hushhhh,* and the doors moved upward, sliding into place above the open doorways. He followed Uncle Mark out onto the platform, where they were soon joined by B.D. and Marguerite.

The station was smaller than the one in Bearhaven, and much less flashy; in fact, Spencer was surprised by how abandoned it looked. The only thing that told him they were in the right place was the elevator that opened onto the platform, identical to the one in Bearhaven.

Marguerite wished them all good luck. "I'll be right here for the return trip. Let's bring these bears home!"

"Thank you, Marguerite," Spencer said, stalling. "It was great. The cocoon bed . . . the oatmeal . . . the brown sugar *on* the oatmeal . . ." he rambled, not sure he was ready to leave the safety of the station.

Uncle Mark cleared his throat. "Can't do much rescuing if we're underground." He glanced meaningfully toward the elevator. It was time to go.

Hoping to prove to everyone, including himself, that he was ready, Spencer hit the button beside the elevator. The doors slid open, and Spencer stepped inside. B.D. and Uncle Mark stepped in beside him, and B.D. pressed a button, giving Marguerite a last little nod as the door slid shut.

The platform rushed upward, carrying them through the sleek hollow space. In the dark, Spencer reached into his pocket. *This is it.* He squeezed the jade bear.

As the doors slid open, Spencer's nervousness fell away, and his excitement returned. He was a Bearhaven operative, and he was a Plain. Now it was time to prove himself.

Spencer stepped out into midafternoon sunshine and found himself standing in a small cluster of trees at the side of a dirt road. He turned back to see B.D. stand up on his hind legs and vigorously sniff the air before dropping to all fours and stepping out of the hollowed tree, confirming that the coast was clear. Uncle Mark followed close behind. The door slid shut, concealing the elevator completely behind a layer of unassuming bark.

"Here we go," Uncle Mark said, eyes locked on the beat-up white box truck that was swinging around a bend in the road.

Before Spencer could get a glimpse of the operative behind the wheel, the driver hit the brakes and a cloud of dust and gravel flew up between them. The truck skidded to a halt right in front of Uncle Mark. He took a few steps back, waving dust out of his face. A second later, the driver's door opened. Someone jumped down, slammed the door, and strode around to meet them.

"Hey, stranger," said Evarita.

37

Under ordinary circumstances, Spencer would never have run up to hug Evarita, but these were not ordinary circumstances.

"You're an *operative*?" he asked after he'd let go. Evarita was definitely cool enough for it to be true, but Spencer couldn't believe that *everyone* had known about Bearhaven except for him.

"Backup," she answered casually, like it was no big deal. She waved a hand toward Uncle Mark's outfit. "That's a good look for you, Mark," she teased.

Uncle Mark laughed, seeming to relax a little now that Evarita had joined them. "That's funny, I was just going to say the same to you." He raised an eyebrow.

"Here we go again," B.D. grumbled.

Spencer ignored the grumpy bear. He'd been so shocked and happy to see Evarita that he hadn't even noticed her outfit. Now, he couldn't believe that he'd recognized her so quickly. She looked so . . . ordinary. Instead of her usual long dress and boots, Evarita was wearing a pair of jeans with plain white sneakers and a flowery pink shirt. Spencer had never seen her wear pink before. Even her usual layers of necklaces were gone. Her hair was braided neatly down her back, and her face was covered in makeup. She didn't look like herself at all.

Evarita squeezed Spencer's shoulder. "Just wanted to look nice for my son Billy here." She spoke in a Southern drawl that was surprisingly convincing.

"Billy?" he asked, but she'd already switched into operative mode.

"We need to get moving," she said, dropping the fake accent. "Grady's been shifting the schedule around all day. I don't trust him not to start the bear baying early."

"Okay, what can you tell us about the setup of the place?" Uncle Mark asked as he led everyone toward the back of the truck.

"He's running the whole show out of a barn," Evarita reported. "And he's got a flea-bag carnival set up outside. Nothing flashy, just some food and a few games and rides for the kids." She tossed the truck's keys to Uncle Mark. "I've got a bad feeling, Mark. Something's off. And I mean more off than a bear baying. There's more there than we realized, I'm sure of it."

"My parents," Spencer broke in, holding on to a secret hope that they'd bring the bears *and* his parents home today. "Are they—?"

"No sign of them yet, my love," Evarita answered. "But we've only just gotten started." Spencer nodded, trying to hide his disappointment.

Uncle Mark unlocked a padlock at the rear of the truck. He rolled the door up and peered into the cargo space. "Nice."

Inside the truck was a dusty silver Cadillac, its windows tinted. Spencer's excitement picked back up. Now that there was a getaway car, this was starting to feel like a real mission.

"All right," Uncle Mark said, clapping his hands. "Let's move. Spence, you're going to ride back here with B.D. We'll pull off a mile from Grady's. You and Evarita will drive the Caddy in, and B.D. and I will follow in the truck. Once we're on the premises, you're Billy, Evarita is your mom, and you don't know me. Until I tell you otherwise, the plan stays the same. You're to locate the cubs and stay close to them. Got it?"

"Got it."

"Good. Up you go."

"But—" Spencer didn't want to ride in the back. He wouldn't be able to see anything back there.

Uncle Mark shot him a look. B.D. was already lumbering up into the back of the truck.

"Okay, okay." Spencer climbed in after the bear.

Spencer strode around the side of the Cadillac to the driver's seat. If he had to ride in the back of the truck, he could at least pretend he was driving the getaway car. Mark rolled the truck door down. In the darkened cargo space, Spencer was surprised to hear B.D. open one of the doors to the Cadillac's backseat. He turned on the interior lights.

"You didn't think I was going to stand in the back of the truck the whole way, did you?" said the bear as he maneuvered himself through the door that, after taking a second look, Spencer realized was customized to be big enough for a bear. The back of the car had also been widened, and all that was behind the front seat was a big open space. The Cadillac's backseat had been removed so that its large trunk opened right into the rest of the car, creating one huge space. B.D. stretched out on his back, his legs extending deep into the trunk.

From his position in the driver's seat, Spencer felt the truck start to move, then accelerate. He glanced into the rearview mirror. *Ha! I'm a bear chauffeur. Cheng and Ramona are never going to believe this.*

38

Spencer moved over to the passenger's seat of the Cadillac, making room for Evarita to slide in behind the wheel. The truck had stopped a minute ago on the side of a dirt road, and Uncle Mark had rolled the back door of the truck up to let Evarita hop inside.

"Want me to back it out?" Uncle Mark called into the truck. "This thing's a little bigger than your Prius . . ." he added playfully.

"I'm sure I can handle it." Evarita started the car. With her eyes on the rearview mirror, she assessed the short ramp that extended out of the truck and down to the dirt road.

"All right, easy does it." Uncle Mark stepped aside and motioned for Evarita to start backing down the ramp. Evarita winked at Spencer. Without hesitating, she hit the gas and reversed smoothly down the ramp at a speed that Uncle Mark clearly wasn't too pleased with.

"I said *easy*, Evarita!"

"Unnecessary showmanship," B.D. grumbled from the backseat. Once the car had come to a complete stop, the bear waited for Uncle Mark's signal that the coast was clear, then pushed open one of the Cadillac's oversized doors to maneuver his way out of the car, and climbed up the ramp into the truck.

"See you at Grady's," Uncle Mark said, nodding to Evarita and Spencer as he rolled down the back door of the truck.

There's no turning back now! Spencer thought excitedly.

Evarita swung the Cadillac onto the dirt road and took off, leaving Uncle Mark and B.D. with the truck, preparing to follow. It wasn't long before she turned onto a paved road, narrowly missing a wooden arrow with *Grady's Grandstand* painted on it. "This thing's like a boat," she muttered, then accelerated past another sign directing them to Grady's.

When they passed a third wooden arrow pointing them on to Grady's, Evarita sighed dramatically. "Heaven forbid anyone miss the place." A few yards later, they came to a fourth sign, and the biggest yet: *DON'T MISS THE PLACE! Grady's Grandstand is RIGHT HERE!* it read, pointing them into a parking lot. They'd arrived.

They pulled into a dirt clearing lined with muddy trucks and other old cars. Evarita parked at the end of the front row of cars, just barely maneuvering the Cadillac into a space between a red pickup truck and the trees lining the clearing. Spencer could see that she'd chosen the spot at the far side of the parking lot for a reason. The huge barn was directly in front of them, so it would be easy to pull the Cadillac up behind it from here. With the carnival sprawling out on the opposite side of the barn, everyone would be occupied elsewhere when the time came to get Ro Ro and her cubs into the car. Or so he hoped.

"Have a hankerin' for a corn dog, Billy?" Evarita trilled in her most authentic Southern accent. She hopped out of the car without waiting for an answer, grabbing a straw purse from under the driver's seat as she went.

Evarita and Spencer fell in behind a family of four, following them around the side of the huge barn to find a carnival in full swing. Stands with snacks and games were crowded into the clearing that posed as carnival grounds, and picnic tables were peppered throughout. A few small, rickety buildings were mixed in among the disorderly booths, their doors open, inviting people to enter, and a handful of dangerously old-looking rides stood in a cluster on the outskirts of the carnival. *Mom would* never *let me ride that . . .* Spencer thought, spotting a miniature Ferris wheel that seemed to stutter and lurch as it revolved. Its highest point didn't even rise above the barn.

The family ahead of Spencer and Evarita stopped at a wooden table at the carnival's entrance.

"That'll be six dollars for the kiddos, and ten for you folks," said the man behind the table. He was wearing a faded denim shirt with *Grady's Grandstand* embroidered over the pocket and a navy baseball cap with the same logo. Spencer examined the man's face. *That has to be him . . .* He wished he could ask Evarita, or know for sure somehow.

"When's the big show, Grady?" *Bingo.* The father ahead of them passed Jay Grady his money.

"Not too long now," Grady answered, dropping the money into a green metal cashbox. "I'm running it early today. Dogs are in a lather." He snapped the cashbox shut. "Fixin' to chew their way right out of the crates if I don't let 'em at a bear soon." The couple thanked him and went into the carnival, shooing their children off to play.

Evarita stepped up to pay Grady. "What time did you say that show's starting?" she asked sweetly.

"'Bout half an hour from now, little lady." He shot her a toothy grin, ignoring Spencer completely.

"Looking forward to it," Evarita called over her shoulder as she ushered Spencer toward the carnival.

"It's about time. Where the heck you been? I gotta get the show started!" Grady said from behind them a moment later. Spencer glanced back. A slouching boy was taking Grady's place at the ticket table. *He's getting ready to start the bear baying . . . Not a good sign for Ro Ro.* Evarita pursed her lips as Grady passed them and disappeared into the barn. Apparently she was thinking the same thing.

"You go on ahead, Billy," she said distractedly. "I'm gonna see if I can save myself a seat for the show."

"Okay, Mom. I'm going to find the petting zoo," Spencer answered in character. He looked beyond Evarita to the big, open barn doors. There was a makeshift grandstand made of mismatched, unstable-looking bleachers inside the building, but he couldn't make out anything else.

He scanned the carnival. Finally, he saw a sign strung between two of the small buildings: *Petting Zoo*. Spencer navigated his way through games, food stands, and clusters of people only to find that the "petting zoo" wasn't much of a petting zoo at all.

After passing under the sign, he followed a dirt path to two outdoor pens. In one pen, a couple of piglets were lying on their bellies in a slant of sunlight, and in the other, a cow and a calf shared the space with three scrawny goats. None of the animals showed any interest in the families trying to tempt them closer with hay or handfuls of pellets. More importantly, none of the baby animals were bear cubs.

Spencer doubled back to take a closer look at the buildings on either side of the sign. The one on the left was outfitted as a miniature fun house, but the one on the right had a sign that said *Grizzlee Den*. He'd been so intent on checking the petting zoo that he'd missed it completely.

He went up the three sagging stairs and through the door, surprised that more people weren't going in and out. As soon as his eyes adjusted to the dim interior of the room, Spencer realized why nobody was paying any attention to the Grizzlee Den. It was empty.

The building was just one room, a converted chicken coop by the looks of it, and half of it was caged off. Spencer stepped up to the cage. The cage stank. He held his breath. There were droppings all over the damp floor, and aside from the door, there was only one window to let any air in. A wave of anger washed over Spencer at the thought of Ro Ro's cubs being kept in such a terrible place. The space inside the cage was way too small for two bears, even if they were cubs. In one corner was a wooden crate with a hole cut in its side, just big enough that a cub might be able to crawl in for relief from pestering onlookers.

"I'd better look," he muttered, hoping to find some sort of clue inside the cage. The door to the empty cage was unlocked. Spencer stepped inside. Wrinkling his nose at the smell, he did his best to avoid the droppings and wet spots.

Just then, the sound of people arguing drifted in through the window. Spencer froze. *Nobody can see me in here!* Standing *in* the bear cage was way too suspicious! The angry voices approached the open door of the Grizzlee Den. There was only one option. Spencer dove into the crate in the corner. With all of his muscles tensed, he landed as soundlessly as he could and curled into a ball to press his entire body away from the crate's opening and out of sight. He clapped a hand over his nose to block out the terrible smell just as heavy footsteps fell on the stairs outside. The door of the Grizzlee Den opened, then slammed shut.

They're here . . . Spencer listened as the argument flared up a few feet away. He recognized one of the voices as Jay Grady's. The other voice was a woman's.

"That bear's a dud," Grady said. "She's got no fight in her. Minute those dogs come running, she falls flat on the ground. Won't get up on her hind legs. Won't do a thing to protect herself. I got a crowd of people out there paid good money to see this show. You promised me—"

"I didn't *promise* you anything," the woman's shrill voice cut him off.

"You said she'd had the procedure," Grady spat back.

"She *has* had the procedure. But there have been cases—not many—" the woman continued, raising her raspy voice above Grady's attempts to interrupt. "If the cubs are nearby, sometimes the implant doesn't work on the sow."

"I don't care about any sow, just that no-fight bear you sold me!"

"Sow *means* mother bear, you dolt. Just do what I told you, and you'll get the fight you want."

Grady mumbled something that Spencer couldn't make out, before his voice hardened again. "It better work, or I'm coming after you for my cash."

"Just do what I said, Grady. My boss doesn't do refunds."

Grady spouted some final complaints, but Spencer focused on the sound of their footsteps heading back toward the door. They were leaving the Grizzlee Den. When he heard the door swing open and stomps on the stairs outside, Spencer slipped out of the crate as quickly as he could. He needed to get a glimpse of that woman.

Brushing himself off, he stole across the dropping-strewn floor of the Grizzlee Den to the open doorway, where he inhaled the fresh air. Jay Grady was already halfway across the carnival grounds, gesturing in annoyance to the woman beside him as he approached the barn. The woman's back was turned, but Spencer didn't need to see her face to know who she was. It was the straggly greenish hair poking out from under an orange hat that told him.

It was Margo Lalicki.

39

Margo Lalicki is here. Margo Lalicki is HERE. Spencer paced inside the Grizzlee Den.

"Calm. Down," he commanded himself. It was already too late to follow Margo. Not like that was a good idea anyway. His job was to handle the cubs, not the creepy woman who just so happened to *also* be on the premises. But the cubs were nowhere to be found. And Uncle Mark and Evarita didn't know that Margo was here . . . He needed to tell them right away.

Intent on finding his uncle, Spencer left the Grizzlee Den, nearly tripping over two little kids on their way in.

"No bears?" they asked, but Spencer didn't answer. Whatever Grady and Margo had planned for Ro Ro didn't sound good. He needed to act fast.

The atmosphere of the carnival had changed since he'd entered the Grizzlee Den. Kids were racing around unattended from game to game, clutching hot dogs or boxes of popcorn. A few moms seemed to be chaperoning whole herds of children, but the majority of the adults had either gone inside the barn or were making their way toward the barn's open doors.

The show hadn't started yet, but it looked like it was about to. Spencer did a quick lap around the carnival's small grounds, scanning the crowd for either Uncle Mark or Evarita. He made his way over to the barn. If he could just slip in behind a group of adults, maybe no one would notice—

Suddenly, a boy around Spencer's age was thrust out of the barn's entrance, accompanied by a loud, gruff "No kids! Out!" from someone inside.

"You didn't have to *push me*. Nobody said there was a bouncer." The boy turned to glare at whoever was attached to the muscular arm that had removed him from the barn. The bouncer stepped out into the sunshine, huge, muscled arms crossed. A football helmet gleamed on his head. *Ivan!*

Spencer backed up and walked a few paces away, then darted around the side of the barn. He pressed his back up against the weathered wood. *First Margo, now Ivan.* Spencer reached for the jade bear. He needed to make a plan.

Carefully, he peered around the edge of the barn. Ivan still stood outside the open doors to the grandstand. Spencer looked at the giant's scariest feature: the football helmet. It wasn't the same one he'd worn when he'd first chased Spencer. This one was red. Did this creep have a different helmet for every day of the week? Ivan turned, listening to someone, then nodded. He rolled the massive barn doors closed, shutting the wide entrance to the grandstand and stationing himself outside a regular door that Spencer hadn't noticed before: an entrance to the barn that wouldn't require moving the bigger doors. Spencer eyed this new option. If only Ivan wasn't guarding it . . .

He needed to find another way in. He *had* to find Uncle Mark and Evarita. Releasing the jade bear, he started down the long side of the barn, searching for another door or a window. He saw some windows, but they were way too high to be helpful. He continued around to the back, studying every inch, when he came to a brass handle. *A door!*

The door was cut right into the side of the barn, hinged so that it could swing open, and it looked identical to the door Ivan was guarding. Spencer glanced farther down the wall. The back of the barn mirrored the front, complete with its own set of wide rolling doors. They wouldn't be any help, though: Rolling them open would get the attention of everyone inside. He turned back to the smaller door, pressing his ear up against it.

"We got us some of the best hunting dogs in the state." Jay Grady's voice rumbled out over the hum of the crowd in the creaky grandstand.

Spencer tried the handle, but the door was locked. He scanned the ground for anything he might use as a lever to pry the door open with . . . *A stick!* He grabbed for something that was half buried in the dirt. It didn't come up. In fact, it didn't budge at all.

"That's weird," Spencer muttered, crouching to get a better look. *Wait a minute . . .* He pinched a piece of what he'd thought was bark on a stick and pulled. *This is electrical tape,* he realized, unwinding the dirty black tape to reveal a tightly packed bundle of wires. He quickly dug around it and discovered three more bundles. After studying the dismantled computer at home, Spencer knew enough about wiring to know that this was definitely not right. *This is enough wiring to power all of Bearhaven! What could Jay Grady possibly need all this for? And why is he hiding it?*

Spencer examined the place where the wires disappeared into the ground. It was obvious that someone had tried to bury the four bundles but hadn't dug quite deep enough. A little ridge of dirt gave them away. Spencer followed the ridge as if it were a trail, and was led into the nearby trees. A few steps more and he found himself standing in front of two silver doors on the side of a hill that he hadn't been able to see from the barn. Spencer had spent enough time in Bearhaven to know that even though the doors were aboveground, whatever they led to must stretch out far below, cut into the earth and hidden from view.

Evarita was right. Something bigger than Jay Grady's bear baying was definitely going on here. Spencer pressed his hands against the silver doors. There was no handle or button or anything that might allow him to enter. He pushed, but the doors didn't budge.

"This place is as bad as the Lab," he muttered. *Or maybe it's just like the Lab!* Even though Spencer didn't think Jay Grady was half as smart as Professor Weaver, he had to give it a shot. He looked around, making sure nobody was watching. Leaning closer, he blew a big breath of air on the doors.

When nothing happened, Spencer cleared his throat and straightened his flannel shirt. Nobody had to know he'd tried that.

He ran back through the trees to the barn and headed for the front entrance. He had to find Uncle Mark and Evarita *now*. Even if that meant he had to go through Ivan to do it.

40

Ivan was still blocking the only open entrance to the barn, but Spencer had planned on that. He headed straight to the Grizzlee Den, grabbing the materials he needed from the ground and abandoned picnic tables as he went. By the time he ran up the stairs and burst into the empty room, he had two plastic cotton candy bags, a popcorn box, a plastic fork, and a plan.

He let himself into the unlocked cage. It stank, but Spencer had planned on that, too. *This'll teach them to clean up after their bears,* he thought, his anger flaring as the image of two cubs being caged in such a horrible place filled his mind again. Using the popcorn box, he scooped bear droppings off the ground and filled the bags.

With a bag of poop in each hand and the fork in his back pocket, Spencer sprinted from the Grizzlee Den, descending the stairs in one giant leap. He raced to the barn, ducking behind a trash can just as Kate had shown him in Bear Stealth training. He stayed crouched, hidden not far from where Ivan was standing.

A loud cheer burst out of the barn. *I just have to get in there,* Spencer assured himself. *The noise and the crowd will cover me once I'm in . . .* He pulled the fork from his pocket and quickly jabbed holes in the two bags, tearing at the plastic with the fork to widen the punctures.

"Here goes nothing." Spencer crawled to one side of the trash can. He focused on a spot beside Ivan's feet, took a deep breath, and lobbed one of the bags.

Nailed it!

The bag of poop smacked down on the ground beside Ivan, causing the hulking man to grunt and jump away from the smelly mess. His footwork was surprisingly fast for a lumbering giant, but Spencer couldn't worry about that. Now was his chance. With the second punctured bag in hand, Spencer pulled his cap down and his T-shirt up over his nose. Ivan looked angrily in his direction. Just then, Spencer leaped up.

As Ivan stalked toward him, Spencer aimed at the cage of Ivan's football helmet. He threw the second bag of poop as hard as he could, like he was rocketing a baseball straight into a catcher's glove, nailing a game-ending out. Spencer's accuracy was perfect. Cheng would have been proud.

Smack!

Ivan bellowed, but another cheer erupting from the barn drowned out the giant's voice. Spencer dashed forward, easily avoiding Ivan's swinging arms. The bag of poop had done its job. Lodged in the cage of Ivan's helmet and oozing bear droppings, the successful hit bought Spencer the time he needed to get through the door and into the barn. He'd have to thank Ivan later for wearing that creepy football helmet. Without it, the bag would have just dropped messily to the ground. Instead, it was stuck in the plastic cage, blocking Ivan's sight and filling his face with the disgusting muck.

Spencer slipped into the raucous crowd, weaving through the first row of cheering people as fast as he could. He needed to put as much space as possible between himself and that door. Spencer shimmied out of his flannel shirt and plunged it deep into a nearby trash can. Ivan would probably come looking for him, and he might as well make himself a little harder to identify.

The people around him were on their feet, stomping and yelling in the rows of bleachers that made up the grandstand. Spencer pushed through, trying to get a good look at the dirt ring in the middle of the barn.

"Ladies and gentlemen," Jay Grady's voice roared. "You have waited long enough!" The crowd grew louder. Spencer pressed forward, squeezing between burly men, ducking in front of cheering women. "I promised you a show," Grady cried over the loudspeakers. "And now you're gonna get one!"

"Gotta be better than last week," a bearded man in front of Spencer shouted to the man beside him. "That grizzly's no fighter."

She's not supposed to be a fighter! And she's NOT a grizzly! Spencer wanted to shout, but yelling at them wouldn't help anything. Instead, he rammed his way past. Breaking out on the other side of the two men, Spencer finally had a view of the ring.

Immediately, he wished he didn't.

Chained to a thick metal stake dug deep into the dirt, Ro Ro was pacing at the far side of the ring. She stopped for a moment to paw the ground and let out a pained cry, then resumed her pacing.

"Let's see if this ol' mama bear can't find her fighting spirit!" Grady cried. The crowd cheered in response. "Bring 'em in, boys!"

On the far side of the barn, two men appeared, holding a metal ring, straining to pull something forward. Attached to the single ring were two chains, and at the end of each chain, with metal collars clamped around their necks, were Ro Ro's cubs. The cubs thrashed and dug in their heels, trying to fight the men who continued to drag them forward. Their terrified whimpers filled the grandstand.

No! Spencer's pulse raced. His stomach twisted and turned. The cubs were only a little smaller than Kate and looked just as spirited and incredible as any cub he'd seen in Bearhaven. How could anyone treat them this way?

One of the men yanked hard on the chain of the closest cub. The animal was jerked forward, and in the moment of imbalance the two men got the cubs into the ring and their shackles attached to the stake.

Ro Ro rushed frantically back and forth between her cubs. They were two little brown balls of fluff crouched behind her, their chains tangling, their panic identical to their mother's.

A bell rang, and four mangy brown-and-white dogs streaked across the arena, released from a passageway between two sets of bleachers.

Spencer gritted his teeth, afraid he might vomit. He hadn't expected four dogs. He also hadn't expected . . . these dogs. Hurtling toward the bears, barking ferociously, the dogs looked underfed, their ribs visible beneath their hides. At least two of them had scars, and all four looked crazed.

The dogs launched themselves at Ro Ro, who snapped and growled at them, trying desperately to stop them from reaching her cubs. She cuffed one of the dogs with a heavy paw, and it tumbled backward into the dirt.

The crowd cheered. Spencer wanted to scream. How could so many people stand here and watch this happen? How could they *enjoy* it? He stared into the ring, his eyes welling with tears of anger.

Ro Ro strained at her chains, shaking and miserable, while her cubs bleated in terror. The dogs snarled at them, then moved in to bite Ro Ro's paws and the soft fur of her throat. They kept on coming, barking and snarling and grabbing at her fur.

As soon as two of the dogs started to drag Ro Ro down into the dirt, another lunged around her to go after a cub. Ro Ro roared and threw herself on top of the dog. The fourth dog leaped on top of her, sinking its teeth into her throat.

"Ro Ro! No!" Spencer cried. He couldn't stop himself. He felt as trapped as she was.

For an instant, Spencer thought that Ro Ro might have heard him. He was sure he'd seen her head flick in his direction. Then, it didn't matter if she'd heard or not. Ro Ro was rising up on her hind legs. A new snarl rippled through her body. She grabbed one of the dogs by the collar and thrust it aside. The audience gasped, then erupted into screams and whistles.

Spencer wanted to look away. The sight of so many animals fighting for their lives was too much . . . too horrible . . . but he kept his eyes locked on Ro Ro, willing her to be strong enough to protect herself and the cubs. At least until this horrible show was over and Uncle Mark, Evarita, and Spencer could get to them—

A hand clamped down on Spencer's shoulder.

41

Adrenaline thundered through Spencer's veins. Every muscle in his body was tense, ready to spring into action. Ivan wasn't going to get him without a fight. Gritting his teeth in a snarl to match Ro Ro's, Spencer prepared to whirl around and face that helmet-wearing—

"Billy, you know you're not supposed to be in here!"

Evarita!

Spencer spun around. "How'd you find me?" he practically gasped in relief, barely resisting the urge to hug her again. The warning look in her eye answered his question. He wasn't exactly making himself hard to find. "Sorry . . . I can explain!" In the shock and chaos of the bear baying, Spencer had forgotten why he'd come into the barn in the first place. Now he wanted to tell Evarita everything he'd found out.

"Not in here you can't, mister." Evarita took hold of his arm, but Spencer pulled back. He couldn't go out the front, not if Ivan was there. He took Evarita's hand. If anything, holding her hand would signal that something was *really* off.

"I think it's this way, Mom," he said determinedly, shooting her the most meaningful look he could manage.

Pulling Evarita along behind him, Spencer made his way through the crowd. It wasn't nearly as hard to move now as it had been before. Men looked down angrily when Spencer tried to push past them, but then they saw Evarita in her flowery pink shirt, and suddenly their path opened up.

As quickly as he could, Spencer led Evarita to the door at the back of the barn that he'd tried to get in through earlier. Hidden behind a set of bleachers, it stood unguarded. To Spencer's relief, it wasn't the lock itself that had held the door shut from the outside, just a wooden bolt that he could easily push aside.

"Billy, I'm not sure we want to be back here," Evarita said, looking around, but there was nobody there to see them. A surge of cheers and hollers burst out of the crowd, echoing loudly in the space beneath the stands.

"I can't go out the other way," Spencer whispered urgently. "Ivan's out there. Margo's here, too."

"You saw *Margo*?" Evarita whispered back. "I saw Ivan on the way in." Spencer pushed the door open just enough to slip out, then closed it quietly once Evarita had stepped out behind him.

"I saw her," Spencer rushed on, still whispering. "I wanted to tell Uncle Mark, to warn him. But, Eva—" She cut him off with a warning look. "There's something really weird going on here," he continued, dropping his voice even lower.

Another roar from the crowd thundered out of the barn. Evarita glanced over her shoulder. "I have to get back. The show sounds like it's getting close to the end. We don't know where they're keeping the bears yet—" She broke off midsentence. There wasn't time to explain. "Go back to the Cadillac. We'll meet you there as soon as possible."

"Wait—" Spencer needed to tell her about the wiring he'd found in the ground and the silver doors that the buried wires had led him to. He needed to explain that there *was* more to Grady's Grandstand than they'd thought; he was sure of it now.

"I can't wait any longer, but don't worry," Evarita said. "We'll get them out of here." Without another word, she slipped back into the barn. Raucous cheers washed over Spencer as the door swung shut behind her.

He kicked the bundle of wires that he'd dug out of the ground earlier. He wasn't going to wait in the car doing nothing. Not when Ro Ro and the cubs were in danger and needed help.

Spencer walked into the trees again. Following the path that the wires made, he returned to the silver doors set into the hill. He pushed on the doors again, but they didn't move. Maybe there was a button hidden nearby, some sort of trigger he'd missed. He studied the surface of the hill but didn't come up with anything. He searched the surrounding trees, running his hands along their bark, feeling for anything unnatural.

Bang! The door of the barn slammed open. Quickly, Spencer ducked behind the tree he'd been inspecting, flattening himself against its trunk. Shouts and whistles flooded out of the barn. The show was over. Spencer peeked around the tree to look back down the hidden path to the barn.

He almost choked. Ro Ro's head was only inches from his face and she was staring right at him! Before either of them could move, the chain around her neck jerked violently, and she was forced to look away. Spencer scanned his surroundings, preparing to use Bear Stealth to escape if he had to, but apparently Ro Ro's handler hadn't cared to follow her gaze.

"Open it already," a gruff voice said.

"I'm *trying*," another voice shot back angrily. "Keep hold of 'em so I can hit the button." Chains rattled and Ro Ro huffed.

"You expect me to hold 'em both?" a third voice spat.

"Gimme a break! *Here*."

The silver doors slowly slid apart, opening a wide entrance into the hill. Three muscled thugs walked through, the first leading Ro Ro inside on a chain, and the other two following behind with the cubs.

I have to do something! Spencer rose and stepped toward the doors. *No.* He hesitated. *Find Uncle Mark and Evarita first.* The doors started to slide shut. *There's no time!* The goons were disappearing into the hill with the bears. *This could be the only chance we have!*

"Let me GO!"

Spencer whirled around. Evarita was struggling in the doorway at the rear of the barn, a thick arm wrapped around her waist to hold her back. There was another shout, and Uncle Mark pushed into the doorway behind Evarita. He was fighting someone off, trying as hard as Evarita was to get out of the barn and follow the bears. Spencer hesitated. The silver doors were almost closed; he had to move now.

He locked eyes with Uncle Mark. Shock passed across his uncle's face. Suddenly, a red football helmet entered the scuffle, and they lost sight of each other.

Now!

Spencer ran toward the silver doors. He leaped into the air and spun sideways, slipping through the last bit of space between the closing doors. A second later, they sealed shut behind him.

42

The bears' chains shook loudly, the metallic clanking echoing through the passageway. Relieved that no one had heard him over all of the noise, Spencer didn't wait to catch his breath. Soundlessly, sticking close to the wall, he crept along behind the thugs as they hustled the bears forward.

Just as Spencer had suspected, the tunnel sloped downward sharply, leading them into the ground. The floor was covered in gray tiles, and the walls and ceiling gleamed silvery gray under a harsh row of lights that ran the length of the passage. There were no doors, and nothing Spencer could hide behind if one of the men were to turn. It was like being in a huge metal tube.

The tunnel flattened out and opened into a wider corridor with doors on either side. In the glare of bright lights, Spencer was even more exposed than he'd been in the tunnel. Still, he continued to follow, stealthily silent-walking as closely behind as he could.

Ro Ro protested with every step, pulling against the chain, swiping a paw at the metal collar around her neck. Spencer couldn't stand to watch the bear's agony, but the trouble she was causing was keeping all three men busy. The goon with Ro Ro's chain strained to keep hold of her, dragging her along, and the goons with the cubs each brandished a menacing-looking prod to threaten and herd the animals, though the cubs had stopped struggling. Whimpering and staying as close to each other as they could, the cubs padded along behind, looking exhausted. Ro Ro's strength was obviously diminishing, too. Spencer could see she was favoring her left hind leg, and blood speckled the gleaming gray floor every few yards. She was hurt. How much farther could they be taking the bears?

One of these doors must lead to the bears' cages. Spencer craned his neck to peer into a room as he slipped by, but he couldn't see much through the half-open door. He kept moving, but instantly realized his mistake. The rattling chains had quieted. The men had stopped in front of an elevator at the end of the corridor.

Without a second thought, Spencer took a step backward and slipped through the half-open door. Right away, he realized this was a whole new mistake.

The dimly lit room wasn't empty. Instead, the very last person in the world that Spencer wanted to see was standing inside. Margo.

Wearing a lab coat and that orange hat, Margo stood with her back turned to Spencer. She must not have heard or seen him yet. Goose bumps rose on Spencer's arms.

Now what? He couldn't leave or else the thugs would spot him, but being this close to Margo definitely wasn't a good idea, either. He reached into his pocket, taking hold of the jade bear.

Margo was facing a long, crescent-shaped console lined with large computer monitors. It looked so much like the surveillance room in the Lab that for a second, Spencer felt like he was back in Bearhaven. The feeling didn't last long. The loud rattling of the bears' chains suddenly poured into the room from the hallway. Sure that Margo would turn at the sound, Spencer ducked behind a file cabinet. He dropped to his hands and knees, ready to move again if he had to. He didn't hear the chains anymore. The goons must have taken the bears to another floor.

Beside the file cabinet there was a long black desk with a rolling leather chair pushed in behind it. Determined to see what Margo was up to, Spencer crept under the desk. He stayed close to the file cabinet, keeping his body in its shadow, and peered out from under the sleek black surface.

Suddenly, a huge screen started to lower out of the ceiling. Margo erupted into a series of hacking coughs, startling Spencer so much that he almost screamed.

Trying to calm his thundering pulse, he focused on the screen suspended above the bank of monitors in front of Margo. Whatever was about to appear there was going to be huge. Spencer was almost afraid to find out what it would be. A replay of the bear baying? A slow-motion recap of the highlights?

Margo pulled off her hat and tossed it onto the console. Her sickening hair hung in tangled disarray. She raked her fingers through her hair, quickly trying to fix it as she leaned toward something in front of her. A moment later, she dropped her hands and the rapid *clacks* of fingers hammering on a keyboard resounded around the room. The huge screen went from black to gray. An image appeared.

At the center of the picture sat a man in an enormous chair. At first, Spencer was relieved. *At least it's not a close-up of the bear baying.* But he quickly realized that everything about the image was disturbing. It was the chair that scared him most. Really, it was a throne that the man was perched on, and it was covered in pieces of . . . *bears.* The man sat primly on top of several cushions that Spencer was sure were made of bear hide. A patchwork of different shades of bear fur surrounded him, rising up the back of the throne and leading to a row of bear fangs studding the top edge. The throne's legs ended in carved bear paws, but the throne's armrests were much creepier. Spencer didn't want to believe it was possible, but he was almost certain that fixed on top of the chair's arms, preserved and hollowed out so that the man's own hands disappeared inside of them, were *real* bear paws, with long curling claws. *Disgusting.*

Margo hacked out another round of coughs. The man in the image moved. It wasn't a picture—it was a live feed. The man lifted a hand to shield his face as though Margo's germs might reach him through the video feed. To Spencer's horror, when the man pulled his hand from inside the paw, the claws went with him. They were the man's own nails!

Margo slapped the keyboard, and suddenly a small box appeared in the top right corner of the enormous screen. The box displayed Margo's end of the feed. Her image filled the center, but behind her Spencer could see the very desk he crouched beneath. He held his breath, preparing to run as he searched the desk on the screen for his own image or any sign that the camera had given him away. There was nothing. The space under the desk was dark. He was hidden by shadows.

43

From his hiding spot beneath the desk, Spencer stared up at the man on the bear throne. An hour ago, he hadn't thought there was anyone creepier than Margo; now he knew he was wrong. *This guy's* definitely *creepier.*

The man swept a lock of black hair into place atop his head with one claw-like nail and stroked the fur collar of his brown velvet jacket. Beneath the open jacket, a silky black shirt didn't quite cover his potbelly, but the man didn't appear to mind.

Spencer looked to Margo's face on the screen. Her expression was sour, her lips pursed. "You're looking . . . ursine today, Pam," she said after a moment had passed. Her voice sounded unnaturally high, like she was trying to sound pleasant, but the sour look on her face didn't change.

Pam examined his claws, then slipped his hands back into the bear paws at the ends of his armrests. "I'm aware, Lalicki," he answered, his voice surprisingly smooth and melodic. "Thank you."

Margo coughed, looking uneasy.

"Well?" Pam prompted softly. "Did you handle the problem?"

"The bear that wouldn't fight in the ring?" *She means Ro Ro,* Spencer realized, remembering the men in the barn who'd claimed Ro Ro wasn't a fighter. "Yes, it's been handled. She fought." Margo sneered, clearly pleased with her work.

Pam waved a hand theatrically. "Good. Though I still don't see why there was a problem at all. The bear had been microchipped, yes?"

"Of course. All the adult bears have been. But—the problem was—" Pam's eyes narrowed as he waited for Margo to continue. "Her cubs are here. On the premises. The microchips aren't always effective—"

"Aren't always *effective*?" Pam's voice was dangerously sweet.

"Just with mother bears! It's the cubs' fault!" Margo whined. "When the cubs are around, it's as though the sow can . . . like she can . . ." Pam gave a tight smile. Spencer shuddered, and for a second, he was glad to be in the room with Margo. At least it meant he didn't have to be in the room with *Pam.* "Mother bears can overpower the implants if their cubs are nearby," Margo spat.

"How many, Lalicki?" Pam snapped. "How many of *my* bears are being chipped without success? Hmm?" He looked away for a moment, nodding to someone outside of the frame.

Margo hesitated.

"Welllll?" the man suddenly screeched, his voice nasally and wavering now.

A maid carrying a silver tray with a teapot and teacup on it entered the screen next to Pam. Pam ignored her, waiting for Margo's reply.

"Pam, I assure you," she said evenly, "this has only happened once or twice before."

Pam held up a hand, silencing her. "I want to see it. Show me video of the bear baying where she didn't respond to the microchip." Margo opened her mouth to respond. "Now," Pam cooed threateningly. He motioned for the maid to pour his tea.

Spencer stared at the woman beside Pam. She was wearing a sleek black uniform, her dark brown hair twisted into a bun on top of her head. There was something familiar about her . . . She looked almost like . . . The woman put the tray down on a table next to the throne, and as she picked up the teapot, a thin gold bracelet slipped out from under the cuff of her shirt. A charm dangled down, tapping the silver tray lightly as she moved to pour the tea. *Mom!*

The woman's face only had traces of what he knew Mom to look like, but even so, Spencer was certain. It was her. Spencer's eyes darted from Mom to Pam, who was keeping his eyes on the screen ahead of him. Margo's scraggly head was down, her fingers flying across the keyboard in front of her. *They don't know who she is!*

Mom extended the teacup to Pam, who was too busy glaring at Margo's frantic attempt to call up the video to take it. She turned to look at the camera, acting as though she was just glancing over. *Prosthetics.* The moment Mom turned, Spencer remembered the drawers full of fake facial parts. It was obvious now that she faced him. Her mouth and eyes were unchanged, but everything else was eerily unfamiliar. As she started to turn her attention back to Pam, Mom's eyes drifted over the desk in the room behind Margo, where Spencer was hiding. *She can't see me!*

Spencer froze, torn between needing to stay hidden and his desperation to see his mom. He couldn't let her leave. Not yet. Not before she saw him and knew that for a moment they were together, and that he was on a mission to bring her home.

Spencer shot out from under the desk and came to stand in full view. Mom's attention snapped back to the screen at the sudden motion, and their eyes locked. Spencer heard Pam's shrill cry and Margo's gasp that turned into a fit of coughs, but he didn't move to run. He couldn't do anything but look at Mom. And in what felt like an instant, it was over.

Crack! Margo slammed a hand down on the keyboard and the screen went black. *"IVAAAAN!"*

44

"Let me GO!" Spencer kicked his legs and thrashed around, trying to break free, but Ivan gave no sign of being bothered by the struggle.

Ivan had grabbed Spencer before he could make it out of Margo's conference room. Spencer had run from the giant, hurtling over the desk and then under it, sprinting from one side of the room to the other, trying to find another way out, but there wasn't one. Ivan had snatched him right off his feet, but Spencer wasn't going to stop fighting his muscled captor. He had to get away!

Standing a few paces away, Margo watched Spencer struggle.

"I've been wanting to get my hands on the smallest Plain," she sneered. "Might as well stop fighting, Spencer. You're not going anywhere until I say so." Spencer didn't stop. Margo dropped her voice to a snarling threat. "Let me put it this way, the more trouble you give me, the worse this goes for you—and for your parents." Margo's pale skin sagged around the thin line of her mouth. "Got it?" Spencer stopped kicking.

"I did good?" Ivan asked.

"Yes, yes, you did fine!" Margo snapped. "Now get him out of here. Tie his hands and keep him in the hallway. I have to call the boss and clean up this *mess*." She spat the last word directly into Spencer's face. He grimaced. Her breath smelled worse than the inside of the Grizzlee Den.

Ivan carried Spencer out of the room and deposited him roughly back on his feet in the cavernous hallway. The door slammed shut behind them. Keeping one hand wrapped around Spencer's arms, Ivan retrieved a length of rope from his pocket. Spencer watched carefully as the giant fumbled with the rope, trying to lash Spencer's hands together while holding him still at the same time. To Spencer's relief, Ivan tied Spencer's hands in front of him. *An overhand knot.* Spencer identified it easily. It wasn't anything fancy, and if he could just lose Ivan for long enough, he was sure he'd be able to manage getting the knot undone.

Spencer knew about knots. Dad had grown up sailing, and on rainy days during summer vacations, Dad would teach Spencer to tie knots. Spencer had helped Cheng practice to get his Boy Scouts merit badge in knot tying, but even before Spencer helped him, Cheng would have been able to tie a better knot than Ivan was doing now.

"I did good," Ivan grumbled from under his helmet, letting go of Spencer's tied hands just as Margo reappeared.

"Tie the hands in the *back* next time, Ivan," she reprimanded, thrusting a wooden chair out toward her brother. "And take this." Ivan shrugged and took it. As soon as he did, Margo raised one of the evil-looking prods that the thugs had used to herd Ro Ro and her cubs. She pointed it at Spencer. "Let's put him with his beloved bears."

"No!" Spencer tried to run, but Ivan grabbed his bound hands, yanking him back.

"You can't keep me here!" Spencer yelled. "People will be looking for me!"

"Who said anything about keeping you here?" Margo croaked out a laugh as she brushed past. With a jerk, Ivan dragged Spencer along behind.

They stopped in front of the elevator at the end of the corridor. Margo pressed a button beside it and the doors slid open, revealing a platform like the one the bears used in their tree elevators, except this platform was suspended by two thick cables. Spencer looked up into the elevator's open shaft as they got on. There was another set of doors higher up. *There can't be another underground level above us. We aren't deep enough . . .*

"What's up there?" he asked, his voice shaking. *Don't act scared.* He cleared his throat. Margo hit a button on the wall of the elevator shaft, sealing the doors shut behind them.

"The outside world, Spencer," she answered, pressing a combination of buttons on a device in her hand. It looked like a TV remote and a video game controller morphed into one. The platform started to lower.

When the platform stopped, Margo pressed a button on the wall of the elevator shaft to open the doors, then stepped out into an empty gray room. Ivan's grip tightened around Spencer's arm, but Spencer wasn't going anywhere. On each of the three surrounding walls, there was one windowless steel door. It looked like a prison.

"Come on, Ivan, we don't have all day!" Margo barked, swinging open one of the doors and putting the device in the pocket of her lab coat. Dragging the chair in one hand so that it squealed against the polished floor, Ivan tugged on the rope binding Spencer's hands. He marched Spencer off the platform and through the steel door that Margo held open. As soon as he stepped into the cavernous, brightly lit room, Spencer tried to turn and run.

"No," Ivan stated, holding him there. "I've got you good!"

A row of thick plexiglass cages made a U around the room. An adult bear sat staring back at Spencer from almost every cage. Spencer's stomach started to hurt. He thought he might be sick. Whatever reason Margo had for bringing him here wasn't good . . .

For a moment, Spencer almost forgot his fear. Ro Ro and the cubs were in one of the cages. Ro Ro's metal collar and chain had been removed, but she didn't look any better. She was lying on her side, licking a bloody patch of fur on her left leg. Her dark neck was matted with blood. The cubs huddled next to her, sucking on each other's paws and making a loud humming noise that drifted over the top of their cage. Their collars and chains had been removed, too, but they were still trying to comfort themselves. Spencer hoped the comforting was working. *We're going to get out of here.*

Margo waved the prod around like a baton, and a large bear in a nearby cage roared. Spencer jumped, immediately recalling Uncle Mark's warning: *A bear in pain is a very dangerous animal.*

"What's this? A Plain that's afraid of bears?" Margo sneered. Before Spencer could swallow his fear and come up with a response, Ivan had dragged him into the only empty cage in the room.

Ivan let the chair clatter onto the cement floor, then pushed Spencer down to sit. Spencer leaped up. They couldn't just lock him in here!

"No, you don't." Ivan pushed him back down.

"I thought you understood. The more trouble you give me, the worse this goes for you *and* your parents." Margo stepped forward. "Would you prefer to be tied to the chair?" *Tied here? No way!*

"No. I'll sit," Spencer mumbled. After a nod from Margo, Ivan stepped out of the cage and jogged back to the steel door. Once he'd reached the door, he turned back, counting something on his fingers.

"Cage number seven, Ivan!" Margo barked. "Press button number seven and hurry up!" A second later, a plexiglass door lowered down on a cable, sealing Spencer inside with Margo and her prod. *The button to open Ro Ro's cage must be next to the steel door, too . . .* Spencer noted, before turning his attention back to Margo, who was slowly walking in a circle around him.

"Let's make this easy," she started. She tapped the walls of the cage with the prod as she circled, aggravating the two bears on either side, whose cages each shared a plexiglass wall with Spencer's. "You have some information that we need."

"We?" Spencer was careful to keep his voice steady. He shot a skeptical glance toward Ivan, who was still standing beside the steel door but had begun shining his red football helmet with a rag, an expression of total concentration on his face and his tongue poking out of his mouth.

"No, not him." Margo dismissed the question. "Now, tell me, when was the last time you saw your mother?" She stopped directly in front of Spencer. Staring down at him, she ran her tongue over her yellow teeth, as if she were an animal who had caught her prey and was about to devour it. Relief washed over Spencer. He hadn't blown Mom's cover!

"Not long ago," he answered. He was tempted to smile, or laugh in Margo's face, but he was afraid of what she might do.

"When exactly was that?"

He shrugged. He wouldn't tell her anything. It was way too dangerous. He'd already come too close to giving Mom away by jumping out of his hiding spot to see her before she left the screen of the video conference. Now that he knew she was still safely disguised, Spencer was sure the risk had been worth it. That one moment they'd gotten to see each other, no matter how far apart or how dangerous it might have been, was enough to make Spencer even more determined. He would finish the rescue mission Mom and Dad had started, and then bring them home, too. Even so, he wasn't about to take any more chances. For now Mom was safe, and Spencer was going to do everything he could to keep it that way. Margo wasn't going to get any help from him.

Margo stared at him, but when the silence continued, she started to get angry. "Fine!" she snapped. "Let's talk about Bearhaven, then."

"What are you talking about?" he shot back.

Margo leaned down over him, putting her face way too close to Spencer's.

"We have your father, you know. I would suggest that you cooperate. For *his* sake."

Spencer narrowed his eyes at her. There was no way he was going to cooperate . . . But what would that mean for Dad?

"Where's Bearhaven, Spencer?" Margo asked evenly.

Spencer swallowed hard. "What's Bearhaven?"

Margo let out a long, terrifying laugh. "All right," she finally said. "You obviously have some thinking to do." Her voice dropped threateningly low. "But you'll want to reconsider your answers. If you don't cooperate, your father will feel the consequences. And as for you—" She slammed the bear prod down onto the ground, then reached into the pocket of her lab coat.

Margo pulled out the control device. "All these bears around you? They belong to me. If I say attack"—she pressed a few buttons on the controller—"they attack. And guess what. I just said it."

Suddenly, the bear in the cage on Spencer's right reared up on its hind legs and threw itself at the plexiglass wall between them. Spencer leaped out of the chair and scrambled to get away, stumbling and off-balance with his hands tied. On shaking legs, he pressed himself into the farthest corner of cell number seven. Margo's loud laughter gave way to a series of hacking coughs, but Spencer ignored her. The bear bared its teeth and clawed the glass furiously. It backed up and threw itself against the wall again, causing the cage to shift around Spencer. The door shook in its track.

"Stop!" Spencer shouted. The bear continued to attack the wall ferociously, but there was no anger in its eyes at all. Instead, the bear's eyes were blank, unfocused. *It's the microchip* . . . Spencer realized. The bear didn't have any control over what it was doing. It was just as trapped as Spencer was.

45

Threatening to come back to continue her questioning, Margo left the cage to rejoin Ivan. She sneered as she punched a few buttons on her controller, stopping the bear's attack, then stalked past her brother through the steel door. The moment the door closed behind them, Spencer lifted his bound hands to his mouth and started tugging at the knot with his teeth.

"There's no way I'm reconsidering my answers," he muttered as he examined the progress he'd made in untying the knot. If Margo thought leaving him tied in a cage surrounded by bears was going to make him change his mind and give her the information she wanted, she was *very* wrong. Working on the knot a few more seconds, it finally came free, and Spencer shoved the rope into the pocket of his jeans. *Might need that again later.*

Spencer knew the cage was going to be incredibly hard to break out of with its smooth, impossible-to-climb walls. Bears were smart—able to pick locks and outsmart zookeepers— and Margo would know that as well as Spencer did. She wasn't going to take any chances. Still, Spencer stood up and slowly walked around the perimeter of his cage, going over every inch trying to find a way out. Maybe he could break

apart the wooden chair and use its pieces as a lever? He got down on his hands and knees, examining the place where the door met the floor. There wasn't so much as a millimeter of space there. Spencer stood back up.

A few feet away, sitting close to their shared wall, sat the bear that Margo had used to scare him. The bear was calm now as it stared back at Spencer. It was as though a completely different animal had hurled itself against the plexiglass only minutes before, shaking the entire cage with its fury. *Wait! That's it!*

When the bear had thrown itself against the wall, the door had shifted in the track that held it in place. Spencer was sure of it. And now, after examining the rest of the cage, he was also sure that the door was the only possible way out.

"If I hit it directly . . ." Spencer whispered as he studied the door, "maybe I can throw it out of its track enough to wedge something into the open space, then I can lever it open from there . . ." *It's the best plan I've got.* Spencer lifted the chair up over his head and smashed it down onto the ground.

Crack! One of the legs broke and hung precariously from the chair. Spencer lifted the chair again. *Smash!* With the second smash of the chair on the cement floor, the broken leg came off. Spencer grabbed the shaft of wood and turned back to the door.

Without hesitating, Spencer ran as fast as he could toward the plexiglass. He took a last huge step, then leaped into the air, slamming his left shoulder into the transparent surface. With his right hand, he jammed the chair leg at the place where the door met the track. The door shook, vibrating against him on impact, but no space opened. The chair leg hit the plexiglass and bounced off.

He'd just have to try again. Shaking off his first attempt, Spencer ran, jumped, and crashed into the plexiglass door. It shifted a little, but no space opened.

Rubbing his now-sore shoulder, Spencer dropped to the floor to sit beside the onlooking bear in the next cage. He leaned his back up against the wall between them, wishing he could talk to this bear like he could talk to Kate.

Then it hit him. Maybe he could!

Spencer spun around to face the transparent wall. He might not be strong enough to move the door, but he hadn't been strong enough to move the boulder, either, and he'd found a way. This was no different! Spencer may not have the muscles of a bear, but there were bears on either side of him, and each of their cages was attached to the one he sat trapped in now. He'd already seen the bear beside him move the door as it attacked the plexiglass wall in fury; if only he could get the bear to do it again . . . Quickly, Spencer reviewed the words he knew in Rescue Ragayo. *Friend* seemed like a good place to start.

Spencer locked eyes with the bear. *"Anbranda,"* he growled. The bear's ears twitched in Spencer's direction. He tried again, more loudly this time. *"Anbranda!"* The bear lifted its head, ears alert, to stare at Spencer. *"Anbranda!"*

"Anbranda." The reply came from behind him. Spencer shot to his feet. The bear in the cage on the other side of Spencer's was on its hind legs now, front paws pressed against the plexiglass. *"Anbranda,"* it growled again.

Just as Spencer opened his mouth to reply, another *"anbranda"* sounded behind him. Spencer turned to find the first bear on its hind legs, front paws pressed to the glass.

"Yes!" he shouted as *"anbranda"* echoed around him. Like dominoes, the message was carried from cage to cage. Spencer counted. There were sixteen cages altogether. Spencer's cage was in one of the two corners farthest from the steel door at the front of the room, putting it close to the middle of the U-shaped row. Fourteen bears stood facing him from cages around the room, ready to respond. Only Ro Ro and her cubs hadn't answered. They were huddled against one another in their cage, quiet and still.

Spencer looked into the eyes of the bear who'd been ordered to attack him. If he could just make it understand, the rest of the bears would follow. Determinedly, Spencer strode up to the door of his cage, then mimed sneaking out through a crack in the side. He returned to the bear and mimed attacking the wall, rapidly shaking and flailing his arms to show that the whole cage shook when he did it. "Please work," he muttered, repeating the actions a second time. The bear watched intently, paws still pressed against the plexiglass.

Spencer grabbed the broken chair leg and returned to the door. He pointed to the bear. *"Hachuk!"* He yelled the command to attack. The bear hesitated, then leaned back and pounded the wall between his cage and Spencer's with its front paws. Spencer nodded excitedly, waving the nearby bears to do the same. *"Hachuk!"* Four more bears followed suit.

Spencer stood ready to jam the chair leg into the space that would open if the door was knocked out of its track, but the door on Spencer's cage didn't move as much as he'd hoped. The bears weren't hitting the walls hard enough. They needed to go faster, to get more momentum. Spencer returned to the wall between him and the first bear. He ran and slammed into it himself, then looked at the bears around him. "*Gal!*" he called out. They watched him attentively; one bobbed its head in a nod.

"*Hachuk!*" he yelled, running back to the door. Eight bears dropped to all fours, backed up, and launched themselves at their cage walls. The crashes thundered through the room. The cages shook. Excitedly, Spencer jammed the chair leg into the space that the bears' attacks opened, but the door was way too heavy. Once the attacks stopped, the door slipped right back into place, snapping the broken chair leg in half.

Spencer grabbed the rest of the chair. He wasn't giving up now. If all of the bears hit their cage walls at once, the door might slide out enough to jam the entire chair into the crack . . . "*Hachuk!*" he yelled again. This time, Spencer added the bears' word for *now*, "*Ko!*"

BAM!

The impact echoed around the room as all fourteen bears attacked their walls at almost exactly the same time. Everything shook violently.

Spencer's cage door was jarred out of place. He managed to shove the chair into the opening. As the door began to close on the chair, the wood started to splinter. It wouldn't hold for long. Before the shaking of plexiglass had quieted, Spencer leaped over the chair, hurtling himself out of his cage.

"Yes!" Spencer cheered as a deafening roar erupted from the bears around him. He took off running. Thanks to Ivan, he knew exactly where to go next.

Right beside the steel door at the front of the room, there was a silver panel covered in buttons. Two rows of numbered buttons lined the sides, and a bigger button sat in the middle with *#1–#16* etched in its center. *It must control all of the cage doors!* Spencer thought, smacking his hand down on the biggest button. All the cage doors began to rise. Some screeched and clattered, having been shaken out of place, but soon, every cage was open. The bears clambered out, blocking Spencer's view of Ro Ro and the cubs. He pushed into the crowd of massive animals to find them.

Bang! The door to the room slammed open.

"Spencer PLAIN!" Margo's grating voice howled.

46

Spencer had gotten this far. There was no way he was going back into a cage, and there was no way he was leaving without the bears he'd come for. Ignoring the chaos around him, he scrambled through the sea of newly freed animals, heading for Ro Ro and the cubs.

Margo hurriedly shut the door and stood at the front of the room, screeching demands as she fumbled in her lab coat pockets. The bears jostled her, knocking her off balance. Ivan tried to muscle his way toward Spencer, menacing prod in hand, but every time he got past one bear, another moved to block his way.

"Do something, you oaf! Get him!" Margo shrieked from the doorway at Ivan, who looked puny compared to the bears surrounding him.

The bears were starting to paw the ground, huffing and growling. They paced and butted into one another in confusion. They reared up and snarled, but most importantly, they bought Spencer enough time to get to Ro Ro.

Ro Ro was standing just inside the open door of her cage, her stance lopsided and awkward as she favored her injured leg. Her cubs were only barely visible, tucked behind their mother's back. The floor around them was spattered with blood. Spencer raced toward Ro Ro, but immediately she growled, warning him not to come any closer.

Spencer stopped. He hadn't expected to have to convince her to be rescued. Quickly, he looked over his shoulder. Margo was finally pulling the remote control out of her pocket. Ivan was getting closer, clearing a path through the bears with the threatening prod. *We're running out of time!*

"*Anbranda,*" he growled, looking Ro Ro in the eye. "*Anbranda,*" he repeated, careful to get all of the sounds right. Urgently, he added, "*Shala.*" He promised her safety. "*Shala.*" He motioned for her to leave the cage. She understood. He knew she did. But still she hesitated.

Suddenly, the chaos that had been swirling around Spencer quieted. He turned. The bears were dropping to all fours, padding back to their cages.

"Wait! Come back!" Spencer yelled.

"Thought you were so *smart,* didn't you, Plain?" Margo waved the remote control. "Get him, Ivan!" she growled. Ivan lurched forward, his path finally clear of bears.

Spencer leaped backward. But before his feet had even hit the ground, a great dark mass flew into the place he'd just been standing. Ro Ro snarled viciously, rising up on her hind legs to tower over Ivan. Baring her teeth, she stopped him in his tracks.

Spencer ducked into Ro Ro's open cage. "*Shala,*" he murmured to the cubs. They responded to Spencer's Rescue Ragayo right away, allowing him to propel them out of the cage and position them safely behind their mother. He had to get them out.

Ivan tried to duck around Ro Ro, extending a muscled arm to grab Spencer. Ro Ro roared, swung out her enormous paw, and knocked Ivan off his feet. Margo started toward them, furiously pounding on the control. But the control had no effect on Ro Ro, who continued to snarl and snap at her. Margo stopped.

"What, Lalicki? Afraid of bears?" Spencer taunted, stepping out from behind Ro Ro. Margo's muddy-brown eyes were full of fury. If they didn't escape now, there was no telling what she might do to any of them, but the only way they were going to be able to make their exit was if Margo and Ivan couldn't.

Using himself as bait, Spencer tried to tempt Margo and Ivan toward him, toward Ro Ro's open cage. "Some football player you are, Ivan. Is that what you call a tackle?" It worked. Ivan swore and lunged at Spencer again. Again Ro Ro knocked him off his feet. This time, her blow sent the oaf sprawling into Ro Ro's own cage.

Margo crept forward, pointing the control at Ro Ro, pounding on the buttons.

No! Spencer sprinted straight at Margo.

"Ivan! Stop him!" she hollered as Spencer launched himself at her. Ivan couldn't do anything to help his sister. He couldn't get past Ro Ro, who was swinging at him, keeping him inside the cage. Spencer didn't hurtle into Margo, but instead slammed into her outstretched arms, snatching the remote out of her hands. Spinning in midair in a move that definitely would've gotten a cheer in a Cougars game, he threw the control as hard as he could into the cage with Ivan.

Crack! The remote hit the cement floor and broke into pieces. Margo screamed as she dove for the device.

Ro Ro snarled and growled, forcing Ivan deeper into the cage. Margo ran in behind them, ducking and weaving, finally scrambling on all fours, desperate to get the remote. Spencer sprinted to the buttons beside the steel door.

"Ro Ro!" he yelled at the top of his lungs. He spun around. She had to move *now.* *"Grauk! Ko!"* The bear backed up, swinging her paws and roaring at Margo and Ivan, keeping them back. The moment she started to cross the threshold of the cage, he hit the button to close the plexiglass door.

"No!" Margo shrieked. She pushed her brother toward the quickly dropping door and the furious bear beyond. "Ivan, stop them!" It did no good. Ro Ro blocked his attempts to escape as the door slid into place, locking Margo and Ivan inside.

"You will PAY FOR THIS!" Margo screamed from inside of Ro Ro's cage.

47

There wasn't any time to waste. As soon as Margo and Ivan got out—and Spencer had no doubt Grady's goons would show up to free them soon—they'd be ruthless. Still, Spencer looked around the room miserably. How could he leave the rest of the bears locked back in their cages?

"I will find you, Plain!" Margo shrieked. "You can count on that! Your parents are done for!"

Adrenaline shot through Spencer's veins. They had to go *now*. Ro Ro and her cubs lumbered over, anxiously trying to escape Margo's menacing voice. Spencer glanced around the room one last time. *I'll come back for you,* he wanted to say, but he didn't have the words. *"Anbranda!"* he finally shouted as he pulled open the steel door. "Thank you!"

Following Ro Ro and the cubs into the gray room with the elevator, Spencer realized that Ro Ro was still limping. The wounds on her neck and hind leg were bleeding again after her fight with Ivan, and she left a wet trail of blood on the cement floor as she nudged her cubs along. Spencer needed to get her out quickly. She needed medical attention. He raced to the elevator doors, slapping the button on the wall to open them.

Once they'd piled onto the platform, Spencer hit the button on the wall of the elevator shaft and the doors slid shut. But the elevator wasn't moving. He pressed the button again. The doors opened. *No . . .* He pressed it a third time. "Come on!" he shouted, startling the cubs. The doors closed again. The platform wasn't going anywhere. *How did Margo make it move before?* Spencer frantically searched his memory. *The remote control.* It must control everything in the building, but now it was lying busted in the cage.

The only way out was up. He knew that much. But if they couldn't move the platform . . . He looked up into the elevator's shaft. He could just make out the doors at the very top.

"*Grauk?*" Ro Ro growled softly. She knew as well as he did that they needed to go.

Spencer swallowed hard and grasped his jade bear. They'd have to climb to safety. He didn't see any other way. He took a deep breath, then pointed up, to the doors at the top of the shaft.

"*Shala,*" he said firmly. Releasing the jade bear, Spencer gripped the cable beside him with both hands, then climbed a few feet up. He dropped back down to the platform, looking to Ro Ro to make sure that she understood. One of the cubs wrapped itself around the cable without hesitating and started to climb it as easily as if it were a slender tree in the forest.

Spencer watched, relieved that he'd made himself clear, but Ro Ro huffed and shook her head. The cub stopped climbing and quickly made its way back down.

No? Spencer told her again that safety was above them. The bear protested with another shake of her head, then dropped down onto the platform on her belly. Spencer knelt next to her. She was wheezing a little. Blood was oozing from her neck, and she turned around to lick the wound on her hind leg.

It's too much for her, Spencer realized. After the horrible bear baying and everything she'd just done to protect him and the cubs from Margo and Ivan, Ro Ro didn't have it in her to climb the cable. Whimpering, the cubs settled in around their mother.

We need help. Spencer looked up into the elevator shaft again. They needed someone who could carry her up. They needed B.D. . . . He stood. *"Shala. Anbranda,"* he said, pointing up again. Ro Ro watched him intently. He pointed at the cubs. *"Grauk. Ko."*

Ro Ro nuzzled each of her cubs. They clung to her tightly. Spencer looked away. She had to know they weren't leaving her here. *It's not good-bye,* he wanted to tell them.

"Shala. Anbranda," he promised, miming someone climbing down the shaft to scoop her up and bring her to safety. Ro Ro nodded weakly. To the cubs, she growled a string of Ragayo Spencer didn't understand. She nudged them toward him. They scrambled back to her. She pushed them again, nipping them gently but firmly. This time, when Spencer grabbed one of the two cables and pulled it toward the cubs, the cubs hopped onto the cable one after the other and started to climb.

Spencer looked back to Ro Ro. *"Shala,"* he promised one last time, then turned to the cable and hoisted himself up. He wrapped his arms and legs around it. *Here we go.* Spencer looked at the cubs scooting effortlessly up the cable. He started to climb.

Spencer climbed quickly at first, trying to reach the top as fast as possible, but the higher he went, the slower he climbed. Thoughts of falling started to creep into his head. They clouded his vision. His arms started to shake. *Keep going,* he commanded himself. *Keep going. Don't think about—*

Then it happened. Just like it always did. The jolt of panic. The terrifying flash of images: metal, blood, leaves whipping past his face as he fell, crashing through branches, and something else. Spencer saw something now that he'd never seen before in the familiar attack of images: *Yude.* He wanted to scream. A wave of nausea swept over him.

And then the moment passed.

Spencer clung to the cable, his eyes squeezed shut. Every muscle in his body was tensed. He couldn't move. He tried to turn his gasps into normal breathing. The thought of plummeting made it impossible. His lungs wouldn't fill with air.

Now what? he thought, knowing that there was only one answer. The bears needed him. He couldn't give up. Not this time. He opened his eyes.

"Aaah!" he shouted, nearly letting go of the cable, he was so startled. One of the cubs had come back down and was hanging just above him, its snout poking right into Spencer's face.

"Grauk?" the cub growled curiously. Spencer looked up the elevator shaft. He was halfway to the door. He tightened his grip on the cable.

"Grauk."

The cub started climbing back up the cable. Spencer followed.

48

Don't. Look. Down.

Wrapped around the cable, the cubs were waiting patiently and peering down at Spencer from the top of the elevator shaft. Spencer tried to take another deep breath. It was no use. Deep breaths weren't an option.

He'd finally made it to the doors at the top of the shaft, but in order to open them he had to press a button on the wall in front of him. Which meant that he had to take one hand off the cable. He hadn't thought of that before he'd started climbing. Now he was sweating, and all of his muscles were burning from exhaustion. The idea of removing so much as a single pinkie from the cable meant risking a long, long fall.

"Grauk, grauk," the cubs murmured, reassuring him.

"Okay," he said, staring at the button. It really wouldn't take much to press it. The doors themselves weren't more than a foot away, but even so, one wrong move this high up . . . *No.* He couldn't think like that. The longer he waited, the more tired they'd all become, and Ro Ro still needed help. They didn't have time for him to just hang around stalling. "Okay," he said again, his voice a little shaky. *All I have to do is push that button,* he told himself. *Then we're home free.*

"Grauk." The call to go came again. Before he could talk himself out of it, Spencer released his right hand from the cable and hit the button. As quickly as he could, he clamped his arm back around the cable. His pulse raced. He squeezed his eyes shut, trying to calm himself down. When he opened them, he saw that the doors had slid open and they were looking out into a patch of moonlit trees.

Thump! Thump! The cubs leaped through the open door and tumbled onto the ground. Spencer laughed. He let go of the cable and grabbed on to the door frame with his right hand, then unwrapped his legs from the cable to step out onto the ground. He pulled himself out of the elevator shaft in one smooth motion. They'd made it!

Spencer sank down beside the bears, who were batting at each other with their paws, full of pent-up energy. Through the trees, he could see Jay Grady's barn looming, but they were far enough away and it was dark enough now that he didn't think anyone would spot them. He relaxed a little, feeling some of his strength return.

Suddenly, the doors to the elevator shaft started to slide shut. *Ro Ro!*

Spencer scrambled forward, trying to catch hold of one of the doors before it closed. There was no handle. He grasped the edge of the door, but it continued to shut. Spencer's arms were too tired to stop it. With his left hand on the door, he grabbed the jade bear from his pocket and jammed the figurine into the last sliver of open space. The door stopped.

"Spencer!" a voice called from behind him.

Uncle Mark!

Spencer turned. Uncle Mark was running toward him through the trees, with Evarita close behind. They were both still in their disguises, but it was clear that in their relief at finding him they'd abandoned their characters altogether.

Spencer felt himself starting to breathe normally again. *"Shala,"* he said to the cubs, who were pawing at the ground in front of the elevator door.

Uncle Mark dropped to the ground and grabbed Spencer, wrapping him up in an enormous hug. Evarita followed, hugging him, then holding him by the shoulders at arm's length to look him over. "You're all right?" she asked. Spencer nodded, too happy and relieved to get any words out.

Uncle Mark looked at the cubs. They'd started sucking each other's paws again, humming loudly like Spencer had heard them do before.

"They need their mother," Spencer said urgently. "Ro Ro's badly hurt. Her neck and her back leg. She needs help." He nodded to the door. "It's an elevator shaft. We had to climb the cable to get out. I promised." His voice shook. "I promised we'd go back for her."

Uncle Mark stood and went to the door. "Spence, did you do this?" he asked, pointing at the jade bear.

"Yeah, I had to keep the door from closing."

"Good thinking." Evarita sounded impressed. "Very resourceful."

"You're turning out to be quite the operative, Spence," Uncle Mark said.

He swung a black backpack off and retrieved a pair of pliers. As he approached the door, the cubs shrank away from him, blocking the entrance to the elevator shaft.

"*Hruk,*" Spencer said gently, urging them to come to him.

The cubs scrambled over, tumbling onto the ground beside Spencer. Together, they watched Uncle Mark put the pliers in the space that the figurine was holding open. He examined the black jade bear, turning it over in his palm. "Your mom's gonna love this story," he said, tossing the jade bear to Spencer. Catching it with both hands, Spencer wrapped his fingers around the familiar stone. Mom *would* love this story—but wait! He had to tell Uncle Mark and Evarita everything that he'd seen!

"About Mom, Uncle Mark." The words started tumbling out. "I saw—"

"Wait, Spence." Uncle Mark stopped him. "We'll have plenty of time to debrief after we get Ro Ro out of there safely. I'm sure you saw a lot down there, but for now focus on keeping the details fresh in your mind. We'll want to hear everything as soon as we get back to transport."

Spencer nodded. "Right. Transport." Uncle Mark was right; this was no place to talk about Mom. Uncle Mark and Evarita may have dropped their accents, but they were still on Grady's land, and Margo was *way* too close to take any chances. Even if she was still locked in the bear cage.

One of the cubs padded back to the elevator doors, creeping up beside Uncle Mark to sniff at the crack that the pliers now held open.

Uncle Mark took hold of the pliers. "All right, let's get Ro Ro out."

Spencer called the cub back again. "*Hruk.*"

Prying open the pliers' handles, Uncle Mark began to push the doors apart. As the pliers opened, the crack between the doors widened. Evarita jumped up to help. Once the opening was wide enough for her to get her hands around the edge of one of the doors, she started to push, forcing it to slide back into the wall. Uncle Mark dropped the pliers and put both hands on the edge of the opposite door, forcing it back. Within seconds, the entrance to the elevator shaft stood completely open. Uncle Mark fashioned two door stops out of rocks to keep the doors from sliding shut again, then he and Evarita looked down into the shaft.

"We have to get her out," Spencer said. "I promised!"

"Don't worry, Spence," Uncle Mark said as he stepped away from the shaft. "Ro Ro's coming back to Bearhaven with us. You'll keep your promise. But you've already rescued two bears today; time for the rest of us to do some work." He clapped his hands. "Evarita, take Spencer and the cubs back to the TUBE in the Cadillac. Stop at the truck and tell B.D. that we have to get Ro Ro up the shaft on a cable. She can't climb if she's got a bad leg. He'll know what to bring."

"Got it." Evarita nodded. Uncle Mark and Evarita looked at Spencer.

"Got it," he said, swelling with pride. He was a real operative now.

Uncle Mark slung his backpack on. "I'm going down to Ro Ro. We'll meet you at the TUBE as soon as we can." He leaned out into the elevator shaft and grabbed hold of the cable with both hands. Without hesitating, he swung himself out into the open space, wrapped his legs around the cable, and started to descend.

Spencer stood up on exhausted legs. The cubs ducked their heads down into the elevator shaft, loudly grumbling Ragayo.

"Uncle Mark?!" Spencer called down the shaft, "Be careful! Margo and Ivan, they're—" he started, not sure how much he should say right now. "They're really . . . angry. I, uh . . . I left them locked in a bear cage."

Uncle Mark tilted his head back and laughed. "Of course you did, kid."

49

Marguerite swept into the passenger car of the TUBE, a silver tray piled high with covered dishes balanced gracefully between her shoulder and paw. Spencer raised a finger to his lips, signaling her to be quiet, and nodded toward Ro Ro's cubs. She put the tray down on a side table and tiptoed over to where Spencer stood looking into one of the car's reclined seats. There the cubs lay snuggled together, fast asleep.

"Little darlings, they've had quite the time of it," Marguerite whispered as she carefully pulled the segmented hood down. Clicking it into place, she closed the cubs into a pearly cocoon. "And you have, too, Spencer," Marguerite said gently. "You should get some rest."

Spencer sighed, exhausted. If he sat for even a minute on one of these cozy seats, he'd be asleep instantly, too, but he was determined to wait for Uncle Mark and B.D. to arrive with Ro Ro, no matter how late it got. He looked at Marguerite's tray. He didn't want to sleep, but he *definitely* wanted to eat. Marguerite chuckled.

"Okay, how about a rest *after* you eat?" she said, retrieving her tray before leading Spencer into the first car of the train.

Evarita looked up from her tea when they entered. "Not tired yet?" she asked Spencer, waving him over to join her.

"I have two sleepy cubs and one hungry one," Marguerite chimed in. She slid her tray onto the table beside them and started uncovering and recovering dishes. Finding the two she was looking for, she placed steaming bowls in front of Spencer and Evarita. Spencer raised his eyebrows.

"What?" Evarita asked slyly as she lifted a heaping spoonful of macaroni and cheese to her mouth. She closed her eyes, savoring the bite. Microwavable mac and cheese was Evarita's favorite food.

"Your uncle has *that* stashed all around the train, too," Marguerite said, eyeing the bright orange food suspiciously. Evarita blushed. Uncle Mark was a health nut. If there was microwavable mac and cheese on the TUBE, it sure wasn't for him. Not that Spencer was complaining. He scooped up as much as would fit on his spoon and shoveled it into his mouth. It was delicious. He wondered if it would be rude to ask for seconds already.

"Well, you two enjoy. If you need anything else, just holler. I'll be right next door." Marguerite gave them a bright smile, then bustled away to check on the cubs.

"B.D. will be able to carry Ro Ro up the elevator shaft, right? With Uncle Mark's help?" Spencer asked through a mouthful of mac and cheese. "Even if she can't hold on very well?"

"Yes, I think so," Evarita answered thoughtfully. "This sort of situation is why B.D. comes on the missions in the first place, Spencer. He's trained for things like—" Evarita stopped midsentence, her eyes focused on something outside the window. Spencer followed her gaze.

Uncle Mark was stepping out of the elevator onto the station platform, holding his backpack in one hand and a bundle of thick ropes in the other. With a smear of blood staining one sleeve of his shirt and the bottom half of his fake goatee missing altogether, he looked disheveled . . . and very serious. B.D. stepped out after him. Spencer jumped up. *Where's Ro Ro?* He sprinted out of the train.

"Where is she?" he demanded, hurtling onto the platform. His voice caught, a lump already rising in his throat. *I promised her!* He glared at Uncle Mark.

"Marguerite!" B.D. called, staying close to the elevator. Spencer rushed forward. B.D. held out a paw to stop him. "Ro Ro's lost a lot of blood and she's in pain," he grumbled. "Don't startle her." Spencer stepped carefully into the elevator.

Her eyes closed, Ro Ro was sitting on the floor with her back against the wall.

"Anbranda?" Spencer growled softly. The bear's breath was labored, and she didn't open her eyes, but after a moment, she replied.

"Anbranda."

B.D. and Marguerite stepped into the elevator. Marguerite motioned for Spencer to move aside. On the platform, Spencer watched Evarita roll a low, bear-sized gurney up to the elevator door just as Marguerite and B.D. were backing out with Ro Ro in their broad arms. They laid the injured bear on the gurney, then swung it around and headed onto the train.

Evarita and Spencer were left standing on the platform.

"She'll be okay, won't she?" Spencer asked. Evarita put her arm around his shoulder.

"She's lost a lot of blood, but I think she's going to be all right. Marguerite and B.D. will be able to stabilize her until she gets to Bearhaven, and then she'll get proper medical care and go to Pinky's for rehab."

"Okay, good. Where's Uncle Mark?"

Evarita started walking toward the train. "He went to clean up. If Ro Ro needs stitches right away, he'll be able to do it. Come on, let's go wait inside."

Uncle Mark joined them in the first car after a while. Goatee gone, he was dressed like the Uncle Mark Spencer knew so well, and he had three bowls clutched precariously in his hands. "Marguerite thought your food might have gotten cold," he said, focusing on not dropping anything. He set fresh bowls of mac and cheese on the table, then sat down next to Evarita with a bowl of oatmeal and berries for himself.

Spencer reached gratefully for his food. "How's Ro Ro?" he asked.

"Her neck's scratched and sore, and the deep bite on her leg is the worst of it. It'll take some time, but she'll make a full recovery." Uncle Mark sounded relieved.

"Marguerite's bandaging the leg now," B.D. said, entering the car. "She'll get Ro Ro to sleep before she leaves her." The weary-looking bear pulled the seat beside Spencer away from the table and sank into it.

"Before we know it they'll be fixing up Ro Ro in Bearhaven," Uncle Mark finished.

Spencer gulped down a mouthful of mac and cheese. "And Margo?"

Uncle Mark shook his head. "No sign of her—or of Ivan. But we couldn't risk leaving the elevator shaft to look into it."

"Mom and Dad aren't there," Spencer rushed on. "I mean, I saw Mom, and she's not at Grady's."

"Then how . . . ?" Evarita began, but didn't finish. Both she and Uncle Mark looked shocked.

"Go on, Spencer," B.D. prompted, leaning in.

"I saw Margo on a video conference with a really creepy guy, Pam, who I think is the boss, and Mom came onto the screen." The story started to pour out of Spencer. "She was serving the man tea, like she was a maid. It didn't really look like her. She's got an awesome disguise, and I know Margo didn't recognize her because she asked me when the last time I saw Mom was, even though she'd just seen her on the screen. So Margo's trying to find her. And Bearhaven. Margo tried to make me tell her about Bearhaven, too." Uncle Mark opened his mouth to say something, but Spencer continued. "I didn't say anything, don't worry. And I memorized the creepy guy's face so that we can find him, because if Mom's there, then Dad's there, too, right?"

It took a moment for Uncle Mark to answer. "Yes," he said. "We think so, yes."

Marguerite opened the door and shooed the cubs into the car. Tripping over their paws, they scrambled over to stand between Spencer and B.D.

"They're a bit frantic, I'm afraid," Marguerite explained, before switching off her BEAR-COM.

"Excuse me," B.D. said, then switched off his own BEAR-COM. Spencer watched as the two adult bears growled gently in Ragayo to the cubs. It didn't matter that he couldn't understand what they were saying. B.D.'s demeanor softened, intent on calming the little bears. Marguerite drew the cubs closer to her, letting them burrow into her fur as they listened to B.D.

Spencer thought of Mom and Dad and the way they called him their cub. A lump started to rise in his throat, but then his thoughts were interrupted by the sound of a word he recognized. *"Anbranda."* The cubs were looking up at him, calmer now. *"Anbranda,"* one said again.

"Anbranda," Spencer answered.

B.D. turned his BEAR-COM back on. "You did well tonight, Spencer. We were all very lucky to have you on the mission." With that, B.D. left the car, the cubs trotting along behind him, and Marguerite followed them out.

"You were right, Spence," Uncle Mark said after a moment. "We need your help to find your parents."

Spencer pushed his bowl away. *I did it!* he thought.

"Does this mean you'll have peanut butter toast on the TUBE for the next mission?" he asked, wiggling his eyebrows.

50

Spencer woke up to the sound of snuffling coming from both sides of him, circling the closed hood of his seat. He smiled. *Sounds like the cubs are awake.* He pushed up the first segment of the hood. Immediately, two dark brown snouts poked in, sniffing rapidly. Spencer pushed the hood up the rest of the way and pressed the button to return his seat to its normal position.

One of the cubs scrambled up. The little bear tumbled around, smothering Spencer with soft fur until it settled in beside him. The other cub raced to the window and stood up on its hind legs to see over the edge.

I must have been asleep for longer than I thought! Spencer realized happily. They were pulling into Bearhaven.

As they glided out of a tunnel and into the brightly lit station, Spencer could see that the platform was crowded with bears. The cub beside him kept his big brown eyes glued to the scene in the station and whispered something in Ragayo that Spencer didn't understand.

"Shala," Spencer replied, trying to reassure the cubs, but "safe" wasn't really what he wanted to say. What he wanted to say was "home."

The TUBE whispered to a stop, and Evarita and Uncle Mark walked into the passenger car.

"Oh!" Evarita exclaimed. "You're up! We were just coming to wake you."

"Yup, I'm—" Spencer started to answer, but all of a sudden the cub beside him decided that it was time to get down. Spencer was overtaken by a little storm of fur and flopping limbs as the bear awkwardly rolled out of the seat.

Uncle Mark chuckled. "Looks like you've made some new friends."

Spencer stood up and brushed himself off. He grinned. Maybe having a few more friends in Bearhaven wouldn't be such a bad thing. Even if they *were* bears. Ramona and Cheng would never believe it.

Marguerite stepped into the passenger car. "Your welcome party awaits!" She winked at Spencer. As though on cue, the TUBE's doors hissed open.

Marguerite switched off her BEAR-COM and knelt at the window beside the cubs. She spoke to them in Ragayo as she pointed to things on the platform.

"Ready, Spence?" Uncle Mark asked, starting toward the door.

"Ready," Spencer called.

Stepping out onto the platform alongside Uncle Mark and Evarita, Spencer scanned the crowd of bears. The maintenance team was already getting to work on the train, calling instructions down the length of the TUBE to one another. Up ahead, two Bear Guard members boarded the first car. Spencer guessed that they were off to do a security check, but he was disappointed to see that Aldo wasn't one of them. He turned to look down the platform in the other direction, only to find that his view was blocked by a handful of bears in white vests.

"Paramedics," Uncle Mark explained as the bears filed onto the train. "They'll take Ro Ro and the cubs to Pinky's."

"Spencer!"

"Kate Dora Weaver! What did I tell you about running near the tracks!" Bunny's reprimanding mom voice echoed through the station. Kate ignored her.

Spencer turned to face the oncoming bear. *"Anbranda!"* he roared happily. As she got closer, Kate tried to slow down, but her paws slipped on the smooth platform and she started to slide. Spencer jumped out of the way just before she bowled him over. She slid to a stop at Uncle Mark's and Evarita's feet.

"You okay, Kate?" Uncle Mark asked, trying to hide his smile.

"Oh, yes! I'm fine!" the cub answered.

"All right, then!" Uncle Mark squeezed Spencer's shoulder as he and Evarita walked by. "We're going to catch up with the Weavers. We have a lot to discuss."

After a few attempts, Kate got her paws beneath her. As soon as she did, Spencer gave her a huge hug.

"We did it?" Kate asked, sitting back on her hind legs.

"We did it! And I needed everything you helped me train for—the Bear Stealth and the Rescue Ragayo and the boulder rolling and the tech! And I climbed! I climbed up a huge elevator cable!" Spencer put his hand up for a high five, but Kate just looked at it. "Remind me to teach you how to high-five one of these days," he said, dropping his hand. If Uncle Mark's contribution to Bearhaven was the TUBE, Spencer could at least bring the high five.

"Well, you better teach me *something,* after all of my hard work!" Kate said, headbutting him lightly. She looked around the platform, sniffing as she turned her head from side to side. "Is your mom here?" she asked. "I don't smell her . . ."

"No, she's not here . . ." He cleared his throat and looked back at Kate. "But I *saw* her, Kate. She's undercover and in such a good disguise that I almost didn't recognize her!" Kate's eyes widened. "She's spying on this really creepy guy who has my dad."

"Really?" Kate whispered. "That's so cool . . . and so scary . . ."

"We're going to get them back. And Uncle Mark and B.D. said they need my help!"

"I told you I'd train you so well they couldn't say no!"

"You were right, Kate! Now, come on, I bet your mom wants to yell at me for sneaking onto the train."

"You bet she does," Kate said as they headed over to her family. "She hasn't let me play *Salmon King* since you left. Do you know how many times Jo-Jo and Winston got to play in the last *two days?* As many times as they wanted!"

Bunny rushed forward. "Oh, Spencer!" she gushed. "I've been so worried!" She looked him over. "Mark says you aren't hurt. You *aren't* hurt, are you, dear?"

"Bunny, the boy is fine, look at him," Professor Weaver said warmly as he joined them. "Glad to have you back, son," he said to Spencer. "I hear you really proved yourself out there. And then some."

"WHAT?" Kate squealed. "He's not in *trouble?"* Spencer shot her a look. She pretended not to see. "No fair," she grumbled quietly.

Professor Weaver shook his head and smiled. Bunny ignored Kate altogether.

"Spencer, honey, are you hungry?"

"Yes, ma'am!" he replied.

"Well, then, why don't we all say our good-byes. It's about time we took you to Raymond's, isn't it? I think a celebratory dinner is in order!" Bunny looked at him happily, waiting for his reply.

"Uh . . . good-byes? To who?"

Uncle Mark and Evarita stepped into the circle, exchanging a sideways glance. "Sorry, Spence, I meant to explain before we got back to Bearhaven. I just didn't want to wake you, and now, here we are." Uncle Mark looked at Spencer apologetically. "Evarita and I have to get back—"

"Back to Grady's?" Spencer interrupted.

"Back home. There's work we have to do to find your parents that we can't do from here. And now that we have your leads—"

"But, wait. What about me?"

"You're going to stay with the Weavers," Uncle Mark said. "Evarita and I will video in for a council meeting in a few days. In the meantime, we'll look into some of the things you brought to light. By the time we speak with the council, we'll be ready to plan the next steps—"

Spencer opened his mouth to protest, but Professor Weaver cut in. "You'll be included in that council meeting, Spencer."

"Oh," Spencer said sheepishly. "Okay."

"It'll just be a few days, Spence. A week at the most before we plan our next move with the council. With your parents gone, this is the safest place for you," Uncle Mark finished.

"You can keep training here!" Kate exclaimed. Spencer looked from Uncle Mark to the Weavers. Kate was right. He *could* keep training here. In fact, Spencer had been planning on it. He just hadn't planned on Uncle Mark not being here with him. He sighed. If Uncle Mark and Evarita had to leave Bearhaven to help figure out how to bring his parents home, then Spencer wouldn't stop them.

"Okay," he said. "If it'll help Mom and Dad."

"Yes!" Kate cheered.

"We can stay a day or two more, if you'd like," Evarita said, looking at Spencer with concern.

"No, that's all right. I think I'll go to Raymond's with the Weavers. And I want to visit Ro Ro and the cubs."

"You sure?" Uncle Mark offered.

"Yup. I'm sure." Spencer nodded. "I'll be fine, and we don't have any time to waste if we're going to get Mom and Dad away from Pam and Margo and Ivan."

"We'll just be over here, dear, when you're ready. Bye, Mark!" Bunny sang, shuffling Kate toward the elevator. "Bye, Evarita! See you soon!" Professor Weaver waved goodbye and followed his wife.

Kate did a little dance. "Salmon nuggets, here we come!"

Spencer smiled, watching them go. Exploring more of Bearhaven didn't seem like such a bad way to spend the next few days. His stomach growled. Especially if he could start by exploring Raymond's menu. Besides, he had to train for his next mission.

Property of <u>SPENCER PLAIN</u>

Bear Facts:

• Not all black bears are black! Fur colors I've seen in Bearhaven: black, dark brown, light brown, tan, cinnamon, silvery blue, silver.

• Aldo says a black bear's sense of smell is <u><u>100 TIMES</u></u> stronger than a human's!

• Kate says bears scratch and rub against trees to leave messages like on a message board. The scent can last for weeks and tells other bears they were there.

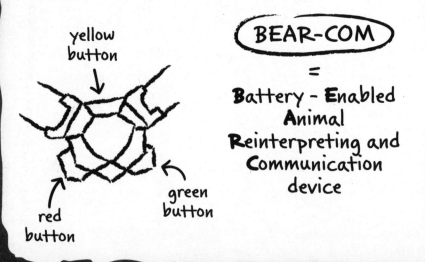

yellow
button

red
button

green
button

BEAR-COM

=

Battery - Enabled
Animal
Reinterpreting and
Communication
device

Running into a black bear in the wild is serious business! If you do meet a black bear, stay calm, back away slowly, and leave the area.

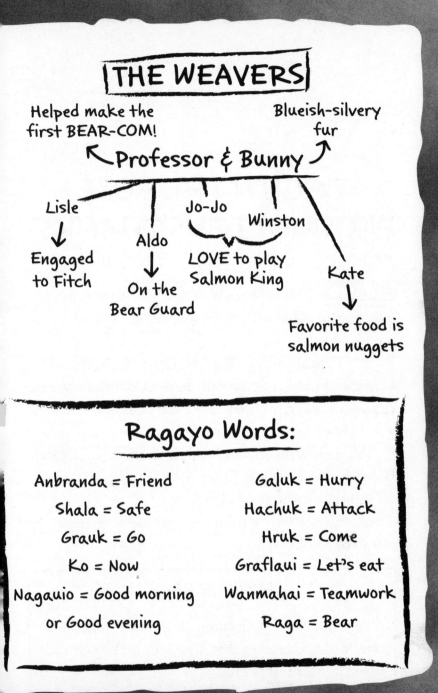

THE WEAVERS

Helped make the
first BEAR-COM!

Blueish-silvery
fur

Professor & Bunny

Lisle

Engaged
to Fitch

Aldo

On the
Bear Guard

Jo-Jo

Winston

LOVE to play
Salmon King

Kate

Favorite food is
salmon nuggets

Ragayo Words:

Anbranda = Friend

Shala = Safe

Grauk = Go

Ko = Now

Nagauio = Good morning
or Good evening

Galuk = Hurry

Hachuk = Attack

Hruk = Come

Graflaui = Let's eat

Wanmahai = Teamwork

Raga = Bear

Learn more about bears in the wild and what to do if you
meet one, and continue the adventure with Spencer and Kate
at www.secretsofbearhaven.com.

EGG IN THE HOLE PRODUCTIONS THANKS:

Erin Black and Nancy Mercado for their editorial guidance, and Ellie Berger and Debra Dorfman for believing in Bearhaven in the first place.

Dr. Thomas Spady, Bear Biologist, California State University San Marcos, for applying his scientific knowledge and understanding of issues facing real bears to the fictional world of Bearhaven.

Dr. Sheri Wells-Jensen, Linguist, Bowling Green State University, for developing Ragayo with her trademark passion for authentic language creation.

Dr. Sylvia Olarte for finding a pie candle and making sure its flames stayed lit.

EGG IN THE H🔴LE
PRODUCTIONS

Egg in the Hole Productions creates rich worlds and memorable characters that draw kids back again and again into series they love.

www.egginthehole.com

ABOUT THE AUTHOR

K. E. Rocha is the author of *Secrets of Bearhaven*, developed in collaboration with Egg in the Hole Productions. She received a BA in English from Trinity College, an MFA from New York University, and was named a Connecticut Circuit Poet by the Connecticut Poetry Society. She has never visited with talking bears, although she often talks to her goofy little hound dog, Reggie, while writing from her studio in Brooklyn.